# Broken Rules

# Broken Rules

*A Novel*

*Addison Paisley*

iUniverse, Inc.
New York  Lincoln  Shanghai

# Broken Rules

Copyright © 2007 by Addison Paisley

All rights reserved. No part of this book may be used or reproduced by any means, graphic, electronic, or mechanical, including photocopying, recording, taping or by any information storage retrieval system without the written permission of the publisher except in the case of brief quotations embodied in critical articles and reviews.

iUniverse books may be ordered through booksellers or by contacting:

iUniverse
2021 Pine Lake Road, Suite 100
Lincoln, NE 68512
www.iuniverse.com
1-800-Authors (1-800-288-4677)

Because of the dynamic nature of the Internet, any Web addresses or links contained in this book may have changed since publication and may no longer be valid.

This is a work of fiction. All of the characters, names, incidents, organizations, and dialogue in this novel are either the products of the author's imagination or are used fictitiously.

ISBN: 978-0-595-46986-4 (pbk)
ISBN: 978-0-595-70710-2 (cloth)
ISBN: 978-0-595-91270-4 (ebk)

Printed in the United States of America

# Chapter One

Abby reclined in her high-back leather chair, her shoeless feet resting comfortably between the ominous piles of paperwork covering her vast oak desk. The intricate stainless steel clock on the wall indicated that it was eight-fifteen. She glanced out her window into the moonlit parking lot and noticed that her brand new Mercedes SL550 roadster was, once again, the only car in the parking lot.

She couldn't recall the last time she hadn't been the last to leave. It seemed the harder she worked, the more work she had to do. She turned her attention back to the set of drawings in her hands and tried to determine what was bothering her about them.

The drawings were a digital rendering of the new aftermarket ground effects for the redesigned Chevy Silverado. It wasn't her design. One of her co-workers did the design and dropped the project on Abby's desk. Apparently, he had no idea how to fix it. The design appeared to be functional. Attachment points were hidden and sufficient to prevent bowing. The parts were seamless to the naked eye making the entire kit look like one piece. Her frustration with everyone had been growing exponentially over the last few weeks. It amazed her that people could do half a job and pass it off as complete.

Ninety percent of the work on her desk was someone else's. She was so busy finishing other people's projects; she barely had time for her own anymore. She could do little about it, though. CG Designs was her father's company. She refused to complain to him about her troubles. He would think that she was weak or couldn't cut it in this business. He wouldn't understand. He would simply say, "Do what you have to do." What did that mean? Did that mean work twenty-four hours a day to get the job done? Did that mean lock herself in her office so no one could hand off his or her projects to her?

There was no question that work was the most important thing in Carson Grant's life. He used to tell Abby that, "People will let you down. If you don't depend on other people, they can't disappoint you." He had drilled this philosophy into her head since she was a teenager. "The only person you can rely on is yourself." She believed his words as if they were gospel and lived her life alone and dependent on no one.

"There's no time to get caught up in emotions," he would say. "The decisions you make have to be based on facts not feelings. Relationships, business or personal, will create emotions, which will interfere with your ability to make clear decisions." He was all she had, so she listened to him. She avoided building friendships and never got involved in relationships.

She returned her attention to the drawings in her hand. She determined that the problem was visual. The lines didn't flow with the overall appearance of the truck. Aftermarket parts shouldn't look like aftermarket parts. They should appear as though they were a part of the original design. These ground effects looked like aftermarket parts; like an afterthought.

She quickly made some sketches, keeping the original functional design in tact, but changing the style to incorporate the rugged, yet elegant features of the truck's appearance. Pleased with her sketches, and in need of a break, she decided to pass the project back off to the original designer.

The echo of her bare feet slapping across the ceramic tile was the only sound penetrating the eerie silence of the deserted office building. Bright, red emergency exit lights served as her only beacon as she headed down the long, dark hallway toward Joe Warren's office. She slipped the file with her revised sketches under his locked door and returned to her office.

It was now ten-thirty. She knew she had a big day tomorrow, but her frustrations with work were making her restless. There would be no harm in heading over to Dreams to try to find someone to help her relax.

Dreams, was a dark, dingy, rundown bar with one crowded pool table that had torn felt and a multitude of cigarette burns. Unfortunately, it was the only women's bar in the area, so the owners had no competition to force them into making improvements. During the week, the dance floor remained dark and there was no DJ. A small TV, mounted in the corner of the spacious room, displayed whatever sporting event held precedence that time of year. It was a known fact, that if you went there on a weeknight, you were there for one of two reasons, either to hook up with someone or to drown your sorrows in cheap alcohol.

After stepping out of the shower in her own private office bathroom, she took the time to admire her perfectly sculpted body in the full-length mirror. She noticed that her thighs were not as toned as they used to be and made a mental note to pay specific attention to her legs the next time she changed-up her workout routine.

An hour later, she walked into Dreams, dressed in her favourite low-slung blue jeans and a tight, black t-shirt despite the below-freezing temperature outside. There weren't many people out on this cold Tuesday night. A quick scan of the patrons revealed five women she had already slept with. Although she could not remember any of their names, she always remembered their faces.

Abby was a regular at Dreams and the bartender had a drink waiting for her at her usual chair at the bar. After fifteen minutes, she was getting bored and beginning to lose hope. She would never sleep with the same woman more than once. It was one of her rules. She was very upfront about it; telling them ahead of time, that she wasn't interested in a relationship. Most of them understood, but occasionally someone would try to convince her that there had been more to their encounter than just sex. She made a point of not telling them anything personal about herself so they would never be able to track her down. For the most part it worked.

She finished her drink, and stood up to leave, when a woman she had never seen before sat down next to her.

"Hi, I'm Hailey," the woman said without looking at Abby.

She wasn't at all Abby's type so she surprised herself when she decided to sit back down and introduce herself. Hailey was a couple of inches taller than Abby. She had short, sandy-blond hair. She was attractive, in a boyish sort of way; nothing at all like the beautiful, young, feminine women Abby usually spent her time with.

"I'm Abby. I don't think I've seen you here before."

"You haven't," Hailey replied arrogantly, finally meeting Abby's blue eyes, with her simmering green ones.

"So … should I order another drink or just wait until we get back to your place?"

"Pretty sure of yourself, aren't you?"

"Uncertainty doesn't pay."

"I think you should order another drink. I've never done this before."

"You've never done *what*, before?" Abby did not intend to be Hailey's first woman. She would never be anyone's first because it would end up being more than just sex. Besides, she didn't have the time or the patience to deal with someone inexperienced today; she was in a hurry.

"Had a one-night stand. I'm more of the wine me, dine me type."

"You want romance? Buy a book or rent a movie. You want one night of hot wild sex? Take me home with you."

"How'd you get to be so cynical about romance?"

"I'm not cynical; I'm a realist. There's no room in my life for romance."

"You sound cynical. Someone must have broken your heart to make you this way."

Abby had no desire to explain herself to Hailey. She refused to discuss anything personal with any of the women she slept with. It was one of her rules. She downed what was left of her drink and looked at Hailey expectantly. "Shall we?"

Hailey considered her response for a minute. There was no question that Abby was attractive and she had gone there for the very purpose of hooking up with someone; she just hadn't expected it to happen so easily.

"Will you at least tell me her name?" Hailey asked as she stood, conveying her answer through her actions rather than her words.

"Janet," Abby replied as she followed Hailey out to the parking lot. She's not sure why she answered the question. She hadn't thought about Janet Jones in years. As she followed the taillights of Hailey's Jeep down the interstate, her mind drifted to the bittersweet memory.

Mrs. Jones was an attractive, married woman in her early thirties. She had long dark hair and voluptuous curves. From the time Abby understood what sex was, she had fantasized about the vivacious woman living next door.

The window in Abby's bedroom was situated perfectly to allow her an unobstructed view of the woman's backyard. A backyard in which, much to Abby's delight, she seemed to enjoy sunbathing nude.

At age sixteen, Abby's father had encouraged her to find a summer job in order to earn her spending money. Her solution had been to do odd jobs around the neighbourhood such as lawn cutting and pool cleaning. Fortunately, Mrs. Jones had been in need of those services.

As she finished cutting the grass one particularly hot July afternoon, Mrs. Jones called her into the house offering her a cold drink. Grateful for the invitation Abby agreed and entered the house to find the beautiful, but scantily clad woman sitting on the sofa offering Abby a beer. "Thank you Mrs. Jones, but I'm awfully sweaty and dirty, I don't think I should sit on your couch"

"Perhaps you would like to take a shower then, Abby?" she said standing up to meet Abby at the door.

Abby clearly remembered the look of desire in the woman's eyes as she approached. She had nearly fallen over when the beautiful older woman kissed her before handing her the beer. The kiss was so much better than what she ever could have imagined. Abby drank the beer quickly hoping it would slow down the pounding in her heart.

"Ready for that shower now?" she asked.

"Um, I think maybe I should go, Mrs. Jones." She tried to protest. She was scared and Mrs. Jones was married. What would she do if her husband came home?

"Now Abby," she said seductively as she traced Abby's lips with her finger, "there are a few other things you could take care of around here before you go, darling, and please call me Janet," she added before closing the distance between them and catching Abby in another lip lock.

Abby melted as the woman's body pressed up against hers. She could protest no further; her body was on fire as Mrs. Jones led her to the shower and motioned for her to go ahead and get in. Surprisingly, Mrs. Jones had let her undress and begin her shower before returning. "Abby, would you like me to wash your back for you?" the now naked and beautiful Janet Jones asked as she joined Abby in the shower.

Later that night, lying alone in her own bed, she remembered how special Mrs. Jones had made her feel. She had been tender and gentle and patient despite Abby's inexperienced fumbling. She couldn't wait to see her again. She was in love and, in the naivety of her adolescence, believed Mts. Jones felt the same way.

It wasn't until the following day, when she returned to the woman's house that her fantasy came crashing down around her. She knocked on the door, and stood impatiently on the porch waiting for Mrs. Jones to answer. After a few minutes, she decided to peek through the window. The sight of Mrs. Jones, dressed in nothing but a robe, and Jack Collingwood, one of Abby's classmates, locked in an embrace, made her heart sink.

She ran home as fast as her legs would carry her and vowed never to fall in love again.

# Chapter Two

"Wow Abby that was amazing!" Hailey exclaimed, reaching her arms around Abby's waist, squeezing her tight.

"Did you think it wouldn't be?" Abby replied arrogantly.

"Well no, but you never know?"

"Look, I've got to get going," Abby said, pulling away from Hailey.

"Already?" Hailey whined.

"Yeah, I've got an early flight tomorrow and I still have to pack," Abby said as she quickly dressed.

"Maybe when you get back, we could get together for dinner or something?"

"Hailey!" Abby warned. "You knew going into this that it would be just the one time."

"I know, I know. But you can't blame a girl for trying," Hailey replied jokingly.

Abby smiled and kissed her on the cheek.

"Someday, someone is going to sweep you off your feet and your whole world will change."

"Doubt it," Abby replied, laughing as she walked out the door and headed home.

She gazed out her bedroom window at the beautiful landscape of moonlight and snow, taking in the spectacular view as Hailey's words rang through her head. *Sweep me off my feet.* She laughed. *Not likely*, she thought, but she was starting to feel a bit lonely lately. Maybe there was more to life than what she would allow herself to live. She had to admit she had enjoyed Hailey's company. It was refreshing to have been with a woman who was intelligent and had something to offer besides a beautiful body.

They had a lot in common, and Abby was dangerously close to breaking some of her rules. She had felt compelled to share her personal life with Hailey although she managed to keep it vague. If ever, there was someone she could befriend, it would be Hailey; but that would no doubt turn into a disaster so it was safer never to see her again. This trip would be a blessing in disguise. It would give her a chance to re-evaluate her life.

She hated the fact that she had to waste three hours to make a half hour long flight from Lansing to Detroit to catch a connecting flight to L.A., but it would probably be safer than making the hour and a half drive to Detroit in the dead of winter. Winter in the southern part of Michigan was always a crapshoot. It could be sunny and fifty degrees one day and then minus twenty and snowing two inches an hour the next day. The variability helped ward off boredom, but it also made planning things difficult sometimes.

"Attention passengers, flight 1342, to LAX have been delayed by about one hour. Please check the monitors for further updates." *Typical*, Abby thought to herself. Not only did she have to fly East in order to go West, but her flight was delayed and she was further from her destination than she had been when she left home this morning.

Finally, nearly twelve hours after leaving her home, she was settling comfortably in her hotel room, thankful for having missed the notoriously awkward meet and greet held a few hours earlier in the conference room.

Abby reviewed the welcome package and examined the generous gift basket, which were waiting in her room. There was a customary breakfast tomorrow before the award ceremony and thankfully, everything else on the itinerary was optional. There were a few seminars later in the week that seemed interesting, but she was here to relax, and relax she would. She decided to take a shower and head to a club that Hailey had recommended from one of her spring break trips. What better way to relax than to find herself in the bed of some pretty, young girl.

As she approached the quaint dark entrance of the club, she felt the sudden urge to turn around and go back to the solitude of her hotel room. She had a weird feeling in the pit of her stomach. There was a strange energy in the warm California night air. She felt like if she walked through that door, her life would change forever. She shook the strange notion from her head and walked in.

It was very different from Dreams. She felt oddly out of place, but comfortable at the same time. Groups of tables and chairs lined the sides of the room. In the far left corner was a sitting area with soft lights and roomy leather sofas. Simple artwork adorned the soft creamy walls surrounding the inviting sitting area. To the right was a dimly lit area with three magnificent oak pool tables. A giant oval shaped bar sat in the middle of the room as if to serve as a divider of sorts between the various areas of the club. Equally as inviting as the other areas, the bar's soft round edges and deep cherry wood tones called to her.

She instinctively headed toward a group of empty bar stools and took a seat in one. Without looking up, she ordered a rye and coke and only when it arrived did she look up to see the most intriguing women tending the bar.

*Stunning,* Abby thought to herself. She appeared to be in her mid-to-late thirties. Abby always did have a thing for older women. She couldn't help but admire this woman, dressed in a sleeveless denim shirt and tight black jeans. She had black shoulder length hair with soft bouncy curls. Her chiselled features and strong jaw line where softened slightly by light freckles. Her dark brown eyes looked as if they could peer into your soul and unravel the mystery that was you.

"Here you go, honey," she said in a raspy voice as she placed the drink down in front of Abby.

"Thanks," Abby replied as she handed the woman a twenty-dollar bill knowing she would then have to return with her change.

Abby watched as she tended to some other customers further down the bar and admired her gorgeous body. She was tall, about five-nine Abby suspected. She was thin with broad shoulders. Her natural beauty captivated Abby.

When she returned with her change, Abby desperately tried to come up with something to say to strike up a conversation with this woman. "So, is this as busy as it gets in here on a Wednesday night?" Abby questioned lamely noting the steady but light flow of people moving about the club.

She answered "Yes" in an almost annoyed tone. Then, as if it was required as part of her job description, she asked, "Where are you from?"

She noticed the look of sheer disappointment on Abby's face and quickly said, "Look, I'm sorry, I didn't mean to sound so cold"

"Its okay," Abby replied sympathetically. Why should she be upset? This poor woman must go through hell everyday, with all these drunken lesbians hitting on her or crying on her shoulder. Besides, who did she think she was? She was clearly no better than the rest of them.

"Having a bad night?" Abby asked sincerely. The woman nodded as she walked away to continue her work.

She returned a few minutes later and placed another drink down in front of Abby. "Here," she said, "this one's on me."

"Thanks," Abby replied shyly.

"I'm Erin," she said as she extended her hand to Abby.

Reaching across the bar, she met a firm, but friendly handshake, and as their eyes met, Erin quickly released Abby's hand and looked away. *Don't even think about it,* Erin thought to herself. *This one is nothing but trouble. Sexy, very, very sexy, but trouble, a whole lot of trouble.*

"It's very nice to meet you, Erin," Abby said in a sarcastically charming voice. "My name is Abby, Abby Grant"

As Erin turned away once again to tend to the others, Abby continued to admire her. It was obvious that her usual charms wouldn't work on this woman, which made her even more interesting to Abby. As she consciously studied Erin's long slender fingers, she couldn't help but notice the distinct tan line around her left ring finger. It had not faded much, probably a week or so. No doubt, the source of her foul mood, Abby presumed.

Spinning around playfully in her bar stool, she gazed around the room seeing no one particularly interesting. *Shit*, she thought to herself. She had been hoping to hook up with someone tonight who might be able to show her around town tomorrow.

She turned back around to face the bar and noticed that the lovely barkeep had once again refilled her drink. Abby winked at Erin through the reflection in the mirror behind the bar as she continued her work. Erin smiled back at Abby for a brief moment. A smile so warm she felt it envelop her like a glove and Abby felt even more drawn, to this magnificent creature. *Get a grip Abby* said to herself, *she's just another woman.* Abby was happy her thoughts were quickly interrupted by a gorgeous young blonde standing next to her.

"Hi, I'm Tiffany," she said with a nervous giggle that Abby was all too familiar with. She was the type of girl Abby chose to spend her time with on a regular basis. They were usually flighty, high maintenance and inexperienced. But they were safe, because Abby didn't particularly like them. There was no danger of getting involved with them. She would not have to risk a broken heart.

"I'm Abby, nice to meet you," she said, as she quickly looked her over from head to toe. She was very petite, five-two at best with large firm breasts and a tiny little waist.

"Where are you from?" she asked.

"Lansing, Michigan. Just here on business. You?"

"I'm from Minnesota. Me and a bunch of my friends thought it would be fun to come hang out in L.A. for spring break," she replied playfully. As she spoke, she casually, but purposefully, inched her way forward, standing now directly between Abby's legs.

"How long are you in town for?" Abby questioned as she nonchalantly placed her left hand on Tiffany's hip and reached for her drink with the other.

"Till Sunday," she replied as she playfully ran her hand over Abby's thigh.

Knowing where this was headed Abby quickly ordered another drink for herself and Tiffany. As Erin returned with the drinks, Abby could see the disapproval on her face but carried on nevertheless. Abby gently slid her hand from Tiffany's hip to her shoulder just barely grazing her ample breast on the way up. She gasped and Abby could feel the young woman's knees buckle slightly under the spell of her touch. How was it, Abby thought to herself, that she could have such an effect on these women and they had little or no effect on her?

Enjoying for the moment the power she had over Tiffany, she continued to toy with her wondering if she had her own hotel room or if she was sharing with her friends. She would not bring her to her own room regardless. That only invited trouble. She would want to spend the night and that would be unacceptable. Rule number one, never, ever, spend the night with a woman.

As she ever so lightly traced the outline of Tiffany's beautiful lips with her finger, she felt her knees buckle once again. Fearing she may fall, Abby swiftly rose to her feet, grabbed Tiffany by the waist, swung her around and sat her down on the stool. Now that she sat there so vulnerable, Abby nearly felt guilty that Tiffany seemed so powerless against her advances.

Erin watched this little exchange in awe, somehow wishing it were her, sitting there, mesmerized by Abby's charms.

Leaning toward Tiffany, Abby gently pulled the golden blond hair away from her ear and whispered softly, as her lips ever so lightly brushed her ear, "What do you want me to do to you?"

Tiffany gasped and let out a little whimper. "I, umm, I ..." she said as she tried to form words.

Suddenly, as if all the cosmic forces were fighting against her, a group of five or six college girls appeared out of nowhere to rescue Tiffany from her evil spell.

"Time to go!" the dark haired one insisted.

"Not now, Liz!" replied Tiffany, completely annoyed at her friends' interference.

"We have to; we promised the others we'd meet them at the party."

"The party? The party, I forgot all about it," she said with great disappointment.

Tiffany looked at Abby, clearly torn between carrying on with her or leaving with her friends and said, "Why don't you come with us?"

Her friends clearly did not approve of this solution, Abby realized as she scanned the expressions on their faces. "Thanks anyway, but I have an early morning so I should get going myself."

Before Tiffany left, Abby quickly wrote down the number for the hotel she was staying at and handed it to her all the while remembering rule number two: never give a girl your phone number. She thought, in this situation, at the very worst, if Tiffany became a problem, she could switch to a different hotel and never see her again. Tiffany in turn, gave Abby her phone number and asked her to call her tomorrow as she walked away with her friends.

The club was emptying rather quickly now as it was after midnight and most people had somewhere else to be before the night was through. Turning back to her drink, which had since been replaced with a glass of water, Abby was suddenly overwhelmed with an emptiness she wasn't sure how to manage.

Erin walked over after drying the last of the bar glasses and said, "Turned you down, huh?"

"No, actually," Abby shot back, "I turned her down"

"Really?" Erin questioned sarcastically, unable to keep her eyes from taking in Abby's muscular frame.

"Yes," Abby replied sharply. "And what business is it of yours?"

"None, but I know your type?" Erin said insultingly. She knew it very well. Back in her college days, Erin had been very much like Abby, picking up girls in bars, looking for one-night stands.

"And what type is that?" Abby challenged.

"You use women. They're disposable to you. You don't care about any of them. You just take what you need and move on," Erin answered knowingly.

"It's far better than ending up like you!" Abby accused, referring to the woman's seemingly miserable state of mind.

"And how's that?" Erin questioned.

"Heartbroken and miserable," Abby replied without thinking. The words had not even left her mouth before she had wished she could take them back. Trying to soften the blow a bit Abby said, "I mean, I noticed you had recently stopped wearing a ring, because of the tan line and I just assumed …"

"You're right," she interrupted before Abby could dig herself a deeper hole. "I am miserable. But …" she stopped to take a deep breath before continuing, "I wouldn't change it for the world."

"Sorry," Abby said sincerely noticing the other woman's sudden discomfort. "I didn't mean to upset you."

"Don't be sorry, I'm not sorry. The last three years of my life have been amazingly fulfilling and I would live through the pain over and over again to have another chance at love," Erin replied, wondering to herself, why she had chose to share this bit of information with Abby.

"Was it really worth it?" Abby asked.

"You have no idea," Erin replied empathetically, somehow wishing she could show Abby what it was like to love someone.

"But …" Abby was interrupted by a firm tug on her arm.

"Dance with me," the mysterious woman said.

"I'm in the middle of something here," Abby protested, wanting to continue her conversation with Erin.

"Go," Erin said with a wink. She knew exactly who the mysterious woman was and what she was capable of.

Abby let this mysterious woman lead her to the dance floor. She was wearing a black baseball cap, which covered her short brown hair and shadowed her face so that Abby could not see it. She wore a black blouse and a very flattering pair of jeans and black high-heeled boots. As they began to dance to Melissa Etheridge's *Breakdown*, the mystery woman wrapped her arms around Abby's shoulders and Abby wrapped hers around the woman's waist. Abby struggled to get a glimpse of the woman's face and just as their eyes met, she quickly pulled Abby close and rested her head on her shoulder.

*Breakdown indeed!* What the hell was she doing there? And, who the hell was she dancing with? She wanted to continue her conversation with Erin, but for some reason, she couldn't break away from this enticing mystery woman. As they danced, Abby could not help but become entranced by her sweet vanilla scent. Her body was soft but firm as she held Abby close. The emptiness from earlier was gone and it was as if, for a few brief moments, time stood still.

As the song ended, Abby felt the mystery woman slip something into her back pocket and then, just as abruptly as she had appeared, she was gone.

Abby stood there for a few moments, completely bewildered before heading back to the comfort of her bar stool. She was inexplicably saddened to find that Erin had left sometime during the dance but she had left a note written on a cocktail napkin.

---

*Abby,*

*Stop by around six o'clock tomorrow. I'll make you dinner.*

*Erin*

---

The note perplexed Abby. She was extremely attracted to Erin, but was certain, based on their brief interaction, that she was not the least bit interested in her. She slipped the note into her pocket deciding to walk back to her hotel.

"Breakdown—no kidding." Erin, Tiffany, Mystery woman. Her mind was a jumbled mess and perhaps the fresh air would do her some good.

As Erin climbed the stairs to her loft, she wondered why she had left that note for Abby. She knew the woman was only interested in sex. That she was incapable of emotion, but she somehow couldn't explain the attraction she had felt for Abby. She wanted to be the one to fill the emptiness Abby was feeling, but would not admit.

Although she and Dinah had split up months ago, it wasn't until this weekend that she was able to remove her ring. There would have been too many questions from her friends and family. Was it finally time to move on? Perhaps a one-night stand would be the cure for her broken heart. Seeing Abby in action suggested that it would at least be a fun-filled night, so what would be the harm? Was Abby even interested in her? She had made no comments to suggest anything of the sort, but Erin could not avoid the constant stare of those ocean blue eyes as she went about her work. But what about Miss Lauren Waters? She clearly had set her sights on Abby. She would no doubt have her completely entranced by week's end, if not already. Tomorrow would be her only chance.

# Chapter Three

Abby slid the key card into the door and headed directly for the shower. Completely exhausted, she wanted nothing more than to just go to bed and try to forget this very strange evening.

She emptied her pockets taking notice for the first time what it was that the mystery woman had slipped into her pocket. It was a blank business card on which she had pressed her lips, leaving a perfect imprint in an orangey, red shade of lipstick. Flipping it over, Abby found a phone number, but nothing more. Bringing the card toward her face, she could once again smell the sweet scent of vanilla. She sighed softly as she wondered what those perfect lips would feel like against her own.

Abby then picked up the cocktail napkin on which Erin had left the note and took notice of the handwriting. So soft and caring. Each character written precisely with great attention and detail.

She carefully placed Erin's note along with Tiffany's number and the mystery woman's number in her briefcase, took a long hot shower and crawled into bed too tired to put any more thought into any of it.

"Hello," Abby said as she picked up the telephone receiver. "Hello!" she said louder. "Jesus" damn wake-up call. *Oh, the throbbing in my head* she thought to herself, as she popped a couple of aspirin and dragged her sorry self to the shower. The spray of the water hurt her face as she wished for some sort of relief.

Oh how Abby dreaded the thought of going to this ceremony today. She knew she deserved the award, but she felt so out of place in the company of all those pretentious snobs. Oh well, she'd muddle through it, she thought, as she dressed in her finest black business suit and a practical, but appropriate, pair of black pumps.

She glanced at her watch and headed downstairs to the lobby for the mandatory pre-ceremony breakfast gathering. Not able to stomach food at this ungodly hour, she quickly snuck over to a corner table as far away as possible from other people and buried her head in a newspaper hoping no one would attempt to talk to her.

Erin woke early as the bright sunlight shone in through the window warming her face. Suddenly, she realized that she had actually invited Abby over for dinner. Would she even show up? Did she even get the note? What should she make them for dinner? What should she wear? Thousands of thoughts ran through her head like bolts of lightening. "Coffee," she said aloud. "No more thinking until I've had coffee."

She gazed around the loft thinking she should clean up, but there was really nothing to clean. She had nothing, since she had not yet taken the time to go back to Dinah's to pick up her belongings. She bought new things as she felt it was necessary, but the loft was bare, she noted for the first time. It really didn't feel like home so she never bothered to decorate. *What will Abby make of this? Surely, she will have some sort of opinion about why I live the way I do.*

She quickly changed the sheets on the bed while she tried to decide what to make for dinner. It was not nearly as difficult as she thought it would be. She quickly decided on chicken breasts with a warm, buttery, rosemary sauce, steamed carrots with rice pilaf, and chocolate mousse for dessert. She jotted down a grocery list and headed to the market to get the ingredients.

"What am I doing?" Erin said to herself. "A one-night stand. I haven't done that since college and, with this Abby woman, no less." She was so arrogant. A trait Erin hated in most woman, but somehow, that's what she found most appealing about Abby.

The ceremony was about to begin as they shuffled to the conference room and took their places. "Welcome to the annual Outstanding Design and Innovation Award Ceremony," the emcee announced.

"It is truly an honour to be in the presence of so many great minds …"

Abby tuned out, as the speaker went on, letting her mind wander a bit to last night. She had so many questions. She should have just left with Tiffany and her life would have remained unchanged. Now, there were questions, there were emotions of some sort that she was unfamiliar with. It made her feel uncomfortable, nervous even.

After what seemed like an endless morning, it was time for their luncheon. She wouldn't stay long, just a few minutes. Since she skipped breakfast, she was starving now, so she filled her plate with food and staked out a place to sit. The only good part of these events was the food. There was always a lavishly presented buffet of every possible food you could imagine. Much to Abby's surprise, there were still a few empty tables so she quickly sat at one of them and began enjoying her meal hoping to finish before anyone decided to join her.

Luckily, she was through with her lunch and already standing to leave, when a couple of businessmen headed her way with their plates. Much to their dismay, Abby quickly excused herself from the table and headed back to her room.

Now nearly two o'clock, Abby would have a couple of hours to walk around town and take in some sights before meeting Erin at the club. She quickly changed into something comfortable and prepared to leave when she noticed the message light blinking on her phone. "Must be Tiffany," she thought aloud as she hit the play button.

"Hi Abby, It's Tiffany. I had a great time last night and I hope to see you at ED's tonight"

Abby was not in the mood for Tiffany tonight, but she would probably not be able to avoid her. She headed through the lobby, out onto the street, and was abruptly offended by the bright sunshine. She wasn't a big fan of the sun on a normal day, let alone with a hangover.

She quickly found a store and bought a pair of sunglasses, and took a couple more aspirin. The sidewalks were less busy than she had expected, perhaps they were busier at night she thought as she made her way through various stores enjoying the quiet alone time for a change. She often hated being alone but today, she needed to think.

She grabbed a table at a little café and just sat there enjoying the scenery letting her mind wander. Why did she feel so different today? What had changed? Nothing, she reminded herself. Nothing had changed. Get over it Abigail.

Noticing the time, she got up and began to head back to the hotel wondering if she should bring something for Erin. Would it be appropriate? Was this a date? What did she want from me? Why was I even going? What could I bring? Flowers perhaps, but if this wasn't supposed to be a date, then they may give the wrong impression. Showing up empty handed may be construed as rude.

She seriously considered calling to make some sort of excuse to cancel so she would not have to deal with it at all. Why did it matter so much to Abby what this woman thought of her? She had never once considered bringing flowers to any of her dates before. Why was this so different? *You're losing it, Abigail*, she said to herself, as she happened upon a flower cart and chose a small but beautiful bouquet of freshly cut flowers. Daisies would be safe, right? Not too presumptuous but not too cold either.

"These will do," she said as she handed over the money.

She decided she should hurry now in case she had trouble getting a cab tonight. When she got back to the room, she quickly took a shower and looked bewildered at her yet unpacked suitcase finally deciding on her favourite pair of blue jeans, a white t-shirt, a denim shirt and a pair of hiking boots. A bit butch, she thought to herself, but after being trapped in a skirt most of the day, comfort was her goal.

She took a moment to admire herself in the mirror, grabbed the flowers and headed downstairs to catch a cab.

Looking at the clock, Erin hurried to take a shower afterward deciding to wear a white tank top she had bought last week with a pair of faded blue jeans and a pair of brown sandals. She quickly dried her hair and headed to the kitchen to prepare dinner.

Realizing it was nearly six o'clock, she set the mousse in the fridge to chill, put the chicken in the warmer, gave herself and the loft a quick once over and headed downstairs to the bar to wait for Abby.

"Hey," Erin said as Abby entered the club.

"Hey yourself," Abby replied.

"I wasn't sure you'd show up"

"Me either," replied Abby honestly as she handed the flowers to Erin. "I got these for you; I didn't think it would be right to show up empty handed."

"Thanks, they're beautiful," Erin responded shyly feeling a blush creep across her face.

"Follow me," Erin said as she pointed to the staircase in the far corner of the club.

Obediently, Abby followed noticing how sexy Erin looked in a tank top. "Those shoulders; my God," she said to herself trying to shake the thought of wrapping her arms around Erin's waist and gently caressing the soft inviting skin that was calling to her. Get a grip, she thought to herself again and began to follow Erin up the stairs.

Suddenly, Erin turned around, noticed that Abby was still at the bottom of the staircase, and disapprovingly said, "Tell me you're not checking out my ass!"

"No," Abby replied, embarrassed that she had been caught, indeed checking out her ass, especially the small rip in Erin's jeans, which allowed a peek at the silky black panties that lie beneath. "I was just thinking about something"

"Thinking about my ass," Erin mumbled to herself smiling. "Get up here!"

Abby quickly gathered her thoughts and ran up the stairs to join Erin who had already opened the door and stepped inside.

"Something smells wonderful," exclaimed Abby as she walked in a closed the door behind her.

"Dinner's just about ready!" Erin shouted from the kitchen. "I hope you like chicken"

"Sounds great," Abby replied as she glanced around the spacious but empty loft. In front of her was a brightly lit but cold looking kitchen. A partial wall divided the kitchen from the equally cold looking living room, which contained merely a sofa, and a television mounted to the wall. To her right sat a simple but elegant dining area, which had been set with candles and formal dinnerware and cloth napkins. The lighting was soft and relaxing. There appeared to be three doors down a hallway adjacent to the dining area. Two bedrooms and a bathroom she surmised without asking.

Erin searched for anything that would serve as a vase for the flowers, deciding finally on a large beer mug she had brought up from the bar one night. "This will have to do," she said as she placed the bouquet on the table. They both chuckled at the sight of this beautiful, formal table setting, which had been cheapened, somehow, by the beer mug vase.

"Haven't had a chance to buy a vase yet, I haven't really had the need for one."

"Looks like you haven't really had the need for a lot of things," Abby replied looking around the empty space.

"Someday," Erin replied knowing that she hadn't furnished the loft because it would mean that she'd have to move on and leave the memories of Dinah behind.

"Hey, is there another way out of here so I don't have to walk through the bar?"

"You've just gotten here and you're already planning your exit strategy."

"Sorry, no, I just … it's well … um Tiffany left a message saying she'd be here tonight and I'm just not in the mood to …"

"Baby-sit," Erin interrupted with a chuckle. "I couldn't resist. I'll show you the back way out later on."

"Let me help you with dinner," Abby said. "It's the least I can do"

"No, no, I've got it, but you could grab the bottle of wine from the fridge if you wouldn't mind."

Abby opened the refrigerator door to find that it was as empty as the rest of the loft. God, this poor woman, she thought to herself. To feel so empty. Abby knew emptiness well, but it was of her own design. She would never let another woman make her feel this way.

"Exactly how long have you been staying ... um I mean living, and I use the term very lightly, up here?"

"Three months, yesterday," Erin replied.

"Three months and the place is still empty? I don't understand."

"You wouldn't," she glared at Abby.

She poured the wine and watched as Erin finished preparing their plates with the same care and precision that she noticed had gone into the handwriting on the note she had left for her.

"Let's eat!" she said quickly changing the subject.

They ate in nearly complete silence causing Abby's nervousness to build. She was accustomed to not being able to get a word in edge wise when her typical dates would drone on incessantly over fashion or some other mindless dribble. *Think of something to say Abigail,* she chastised herself.

"Dinner is fabulous. I can't think of the last time someone took the time to cook for me. Jesus, it was probably my mother, over ten years ago."

"That's incredibly sad, Abby," she said as their eyes met. *Her eyes can't be that blue* Erin thought to herself. They looked like they were dancing as the flicker of the candle shone in them. Erin quickly shook that image from her head and looked back down at her nearly finished meal.

"Cooking is the one true love I have left and unfortunately, I have no one to cook for so this was as much of a treat for me as it was for you." She stood to clear their plates from the table. "Thanks again for showing up."

"Thanks for inviting me." She was surprised at what an enjoyable time she'd had so far. Everything seemed so natural between them; it was as if they had been long time friends.

"Tell me about her," Abby shouted into the kitchen.

"Who?"

"Your ex, of course; the woman who has put you in this miserable state."

"There's nothing to tell really. It's just over," Erin replied as she brought out the chocolate mousse.

Abby could tell she was lying, but didn't want to push the issue so she tried to lighten the mood a bit. "Chocolate, wine, candles, hum ... If I didn't know better I'd think you were trying to seduce me Erin ... Erin ... what is your last name anyway?"

"Davis, Erin Davis, and how do you know that's not my plan?" she said as she gazed into Abby's eyes causing Abby's heart to skip a beat. She felt a sudden tingly warmth envelop her entire body as her heart began to pound so hard against her chest she was certain Erin could hear it from across the table. *Too much wine, get a grip*, she said to herself as she quickly pulled her eyes from the brown ones, which had been holding hers captive for what seemed to be an eternity.

She quickly began to eat her dessert. Hopefully, Erin would not notice how flustered she had become. *When you get home, Abigail, you are going to a doctor. There must be something wrong with you.*

"This is divine, so rich in flavour but so light and creamy in texture," Abby said trying to change the subject again.

"It's heaven," Erin added as she took another spoonful.

Abby could not help but stare as Erin's lips caressed the spoon clearly enjoying the sweet chocolate. She was beautiful, naturally beautiful. Her skin looked so soft. She just wanted to lean across the table and kiss her. *Whoa*, she said to herself. Remember your rules.

"Something wrong?" Erin asked, "You haven't finished your dessert."

"No, I was just deep in thought"

"Good thoughts, I hope"

"So have you lived around here all your life?" Abby asked desperate to change the subject.

"No, not really, my family is from San Bernardino. My parents still live there, but my older brother moved to North Dakota with his wife and kids when I was eleven, and my sister and I moved here about ten years ago. She got married and had a couple of kids and moved back to San Bernardino to be closer to my parents a couple of years ago. We still see each other though. I am required to visit my parents at least every other weekend or they'll send the National Guard out to find me."

"You seem really close with your family, it must be nice"

"Yeah, but sometimes, they just interfere too much, but I know it's just because they love me, and no matter what, they'll always be there for me."

"What about your family, Abby?"

"Not much to speak of. Only child. Mom left when I was sixteen. I guess she couldn't handle my dad anymore. I haven't seen or heard from her in over ten years. My dad did the best he could to raise me. He took me under his wing at his business and has made me very successful in that regard, but otherwise we're not close. We don't speak about anything other than work or maybe to compare notes on our flavour of the week."

"What about friends. Surely, you have friends you can turn to when you need to talk things out." Erin asked as she took Abby's dessert plate to the kitchen and returned to refill her glass of wine.

"No, I mean there are a couple of guys I hang out with and play pool with and stuff, but no close friends. The line between friends and lovers is much too easily crossed with disastrous results." Abby repeated rule number five to herself: Never make friends with anyone you might consider sleeping with.

"You're pathetic, you know that. Is that all you ever think about? There's so much more to life than sex."

"Pathetic—maybe to you, but I am quite content with my life as it is. There's no drama! No problems. I've got nothing to lose."

"Also, nothing to gain. Don't you ever miss waking up in someone's loving arms or just holding hands as you sit and watch a movie on a lazy Saturday afternoon?"

"I wouldn't know. I've never done it."

"Never?"

"Never. I enjoy being alone. I work a lot and I like my own space and not having anyone to answer to."

"Except yourself," Erin challenged.

"Myself is quite happy with myself, thank you," Abby replied sharply trying to disguise the fact that Erin had hit a nerve with that last statement. For the last few weeks, Abby had been searching for something or someone to fill the emptiness she'd been feeling. She just didn't feel whole anymore. There was something missing, but she could not put her finger on what it was. Was she really longing for friendship or companionship? She thought it wasn't part of her genetic makeup, but maybe it was.

"What about yourself? You can't tell me that this … that you, are happy?"

"I'm not happy, not now of course, but I was for a long time and I will be again … eventually," Erin explained as a tear fell to her cheek. The last thing she wanted to do was cry in front of Abby. This was ridiculous. How could she still feel so hurt after all this time? And even more disturbing, why was she talking to Abby about it?

"Tell me about her, Erin," Abby urged, sympathetically watching the tears streaming down her face.

"I can't, I just can't talk about it. I was such a fool."

"Look, we don't know each other and I'll be gone in a few days so you can tell me anything," Abby said reaching out for Erin's hand and gently squeezing it not ever remembering a time before when she'd felt the need to try and comfort another woman.

"It was three months ago. I left work early because it was dead in here and I had been tired from being out late the night before. I noticed my best friend's car in the driveway, but thought nothing of it, since she often stayed with us during the week instead of driving back to El Toro after work." She squeezed Abby's hand tightly now and continued, "When I walked in, I found them in bed together. Apparently, it had been going on for some time, but in that moment, my whole world collapsed. Not only did I lose my lover, but I no longer had my best friend's shoulder to cry on." Erin suddenly shook free of Abby's hand and headed angrily to the kitchen. Talking about it had brought back the anger that had been overshadowed, for a long time, with self-pity.

# *Chapter Four*

Abby rose quickly to follow Erin to the kitchen where she found her facing out the window sobbing. Unsure of what emotion was causing her to feel so compassionate about this woman, her body instinctively walked over and she wrapped her arms around Erin and held her tight.

Erin relaxed into Abby's strong arms and they remained that way for several minutes. Suddenly, as if she had just realized where she was, Erin broke free of Abby's hold and stepped away, amazed at how good it felt just to be held, but reminding herself that tonight was not about comfort, it was just about sex.

"I'm sorry," she said. "I just haven't really talked about it, and it's still very painful."

"Maybe you should talk about it. You might feel better after, and I've got nowhere to be."

"You're being awfully sweet. What happened to the arrogant, emotionless, uncaring, insensitive, womanizer I met yesterday?" She hadn't meant to sound callous, but the words escaped her before she could stop them.

"If you disliked me so much, why did you invite me to dinner?" She wanted to be angry and hurt, but the truth was the truth.

"I honestly don't know; but for some reason, I'm very glad I did," Erin smiled gently acknowledging that her words were not meant to hurt Abby, but to point out the facts.

Not knowing what to say next, Abby grabbed their wine glasses, refilled them and ushered Erin into the living room. "I love this window, the view of the city is amazing," Abby exclaimed.

"I guess it is. I hadn't noticed before," Erin said realizing that she had never really just looked out over the city. The view was indeed spectacular. But not as spectacular, as the view of Abby, standing in her living room. She blushed as she tried to picture what Abby would look like without clothes. She would probably not be disappointed.

"What more can I tell you?" Erin asked nearly downing her entire glass of wine before taking a seat next to Abby on the couch.

"The ring? There's no way that tan line is more than a week old," Abby accused as she stepped away momentarily to refill Erin's glass.

"At first I was too embarrassed to tell my family and friends what had happened. They always said Dinah was all wrong for me and that I could do better. So, I wore it around for two months and pretended everything was fine. Then, after I got over the anger, I started to wonder if maybe she would come back to me. Maybe she just needed to get Carly out of her system. It wasn't until this past weekend at my parent's house that I finally realized she wasn't coming back and that I really didn't want her back. I told my family that it was over and threw the ring in a large pond on my parent's property."

Abby got up and knelt down in front of Erin, gently lifting her chin so there eyes met and said, "I can't pretend to know how you are feeling, but," she took the glass from Erin's hand and set it on the floor, "I can help you to forget if you want me to."

Erin's hands were trembling as she reached for Abby's arm and led her to the bedroom.

Abby inched closer, looking into her eyes, wanting so badly to make the hurt go away. She reached up and gently pushed the hair from Erin's face and pulled her close. As they kissed, Abby was overwhelmed with emotion. Her lips were so soft. Her kiss was so passionate. Abby felt as though she had never truly been kissed before and it felt wonderful. Abby slowly walked Erin backward toward the bed. Her heart melted when she saw the tears welling up in Erin's eyes.

"I'm sorry … I can't … This wasn't … I wasn't supposed to feel … It was just supposed to be sex, I'm so sorry …" Erin said as she began to sob again, realizing that instead of just a one night stand with a woman she didn't know or didn't care to know, this night had turned out to be much more. So much more, that Erin could not wrap her head around what she was feeling that moment.

"It's okay," Abby whispered, pulling Erin close and holding her, surprised at her own relief. For the first time in her life, she really questioned whether or not she would hate herself for taking advantage of someone. Erin had made it clear that she wanted Abby, and Abby certainly wanted Erin, but there was something more, something she could not explain.

Abby woke early. It was only 5:00 AM, but she was still functioning on Eastern Standard Time. She smiled for a moment at Erin who slept peacefully in her arms. *Shit!* She said to herself as she quietly unravelled herself from Erin. *Idiot! What did you do?* She hadn't even bothered to undress last night as Erin lay in her arms so peacefully she didn't want to wake her, but she certainly didn't mean to fall asleep as well. She had planned to wait a few more minutes before making her escape back to her hotel room for the night, but she fell asleep. *Now what? Never, ever spend the night. You know the rules.*

She grabbed her boots and quietly headed out to the street before taking the time to put them on. She was walking fast, nearly running by the time she got back to the hotel. She took a long, hot shower, a sleeping pill and went directly to bed trying to erase the wonderful memory of waking up in Erin's bed from her mind.

Erin woke to the bright sunlight flooding through the window. She smiled as she remembered how good it felt to be in Abby's arms. And for once, in what had seemed like forever, Dinah was not the first person she thought of when she woke. She rolled over hoping to catch a glimpse of Abby sleeping. Her heart sank when she realized she was alone.

She darted out of bed hoping to find her in the kitchen, but she was gone, not even a note. Shit! Did she really expect anything different from her? Remembering the kiss from the night before, Erin brought her fingers to her lips and her thoughts flashed back to the look in Abby's eyes as they looked back at her with such tenderness. The look on her face indicated that Erin was more than just Abby's next conquest. So, why did she leave? Fear? She had clearly spent most of the night as Erin had awakened three or four times during the night to find Abby's strong arms still wrapped tightly around her.

As memories of last night ran through her mind, she wrapped her own arms around herself and sighed. Never before had she felt so safe and secure in a woman's arms. Get over it Erin, she's gone. *Two nights ago, you couldn't bear to be in her presence and now you're longing for her to hold you. And why? What had changed?* Had it just been that she was able to bear her soul about Dinah, or was just a purely physical attraction. That body, those eyes, my God! She gave her head a shake to try to erase the visions from her mind.

"Hello!" Abby said in a sleepy voice as she answered the phone.

"Hi Abby, it's Tiffany."

"Hey, Tiffany!" Abby replied glaring at the clock realizing that she had slept the whole day and it was nearly 5:00 PM. "What's up?"

"I just wanted to let you know that my friends and I are headed to Santa Monica for the night and we won't be back until tomorrow afternoon."

"Oh! Okay. Have a good time. Maybe we can get together tomorrow night then." Abby asked hoping to use Tiffany as a diversion for the unwelcome feelings she was having about Erin.

"That sounds great! See you then!"

Abby wiped the sleep from her eyes and found her thoughts wandering to Erin. She reached for the shirt she wore last night, which she had casually thrown on the bed that morning, and brought it to her face. Inhaling the beautiful aroma that still lingered on it caused a flood of memories to come rushing back to her. The unique scent of wind, rain and passion was intoxicating. She remembered how comforting it was to wake up next to Erin. As if, she belonged there. She suddenly wanted to run back to her and just hold her. It wasn't sexual, although she found Erin to be incredibly sexy. It was something more. She just wanted to see her again and be with her. Just be! *Okay Abigail, you've finally lost it ... what is it about this woman? Suddenly you are breaking your rules and longing for a woman you don't even know. Get over it! Move on!*

Since Tiffany was not available to serve as a distraction, Abby reached for her briefcase and fished through it until she found the mystery woman's phone number. *Maybe she will help get your mind off Erin.* She dialled the number and anxiously tapped her finger on the desk while it rang.

"Yes, may I help you?" The voice on the other end of the phone said.

"I um ... someone, you perhaps? Gave me this number the other night at ED's."

"I thought I might hear from you! Are you free for dinner?"

"As a matter of fact, I am!" Abby replied eagerly realizing she hadn't eaten in nearly twenty-four hours.

"Okay then, I'll send a car for you in an hour. You're staying at the Hyatt right?"

"Yes, but I don't even ..." Click. She was interrupted mid-sentence by the dial tone. Still, Abby had no idea who this woman was. And to send a car for her? How strange. This should be an interesting evening, she thought to herself as she quickly headed for the shower. She dressed in the only remaining clean clothes that she had making a mental note to send everything out to be cleaned tomorrow before meeting up with Tiffany.

While she waited in the lobby, she wondered how she would even know what kind of car to look for. Then suddenly, at six o'clock sharp, a black limo pulled up and the driver approached saying, "Madam, I believe I am your ride." He led her to the door and held it open as she got in.

"Where are we headed?" Abby asked after they had been driving for a few minutes.

"I'm sorry, but I'm not a liberty to discuss that with you, Madam"

"My name is Abby, you do not have to call me Madam," she said feeling both annoyed and now a little bit scared. Where was she and where the hell was she headed?

"I understand, Madam. We shall arrive in approximately fifteen minutes."

"Arrive where?" she said under her breath. They had been heading away from the city for about twenty minutes down a bunch of back roads that seemed to lead to nowhere.

Finally, after what felt like an hour, they turned down a road that appeared to be at least civilized. Abby took note of the name of the road. Fox Run Drive. No Exit. *Great! A dead end. How appropriate.*

There was a security booth at the end of the road, but they were immediately ushered past it. The driveway seemed to go on for miles through dense brush until they finally reached the house. Well, it wasn't so much a house as it was a mansion. It was huge. Abby had been to extravagant homes before, but this.... this was surely something that had been viewed by the likes of Robin Leach at some point.

"Madam," said the driver as he opened the door motioning for her to exit.

"Abby," she corrected him "Who lives here?"

"Not at liberty to say, Madam."

Who was he, the secret service? Jesus!

Suddenly feeling very underdressed, in her torn jeans and white denim shirt, she thought about asking the driver to take her back to the hotel, but he had already pulled away. She had not yet reached the top step when a butler opened the front door and said, "Please come in. Miss Lauren is tied up on a conference call, but she shouldn't be but a few more moments."

"Can I get you a drink?" he asked as he ushered her to what appeared to be a library.

*Miss Lauren?* She thought to herself.

"I would like a glass of water, please, if it wouldn't be too much trouble?"

"No trouble at all, Madam. I shall bring it right out to you. Please make yourself comfortable."

She glanced around the room wondering who Lauren was and it wasn't until she noticed the Oscar sitting on the mantel that she realized she was in Lauren Waters' house. *Oh my God!* She loved all of her movies and she had secretly fantasized about Lauren for years. But what did she want with Abby and what did Lauren have to do with the woman from ED's the other night?

"Here is your water, Madam. Miss Lauren shall be with you momentarily."

"Thank-you," Abby replied, wishing that she had asked for something stronger.

"Sorry to keep you waiting!" Lauren exclaimed as she entered the room dressed in a comfortable pair of baggy jeans and a lacy pink top. Her perfect long blond hair was pulled back into a ponytail. "Hi! I'm Lauren, it's a pleasure to meet you!" she said as she extended her hand to Abby.

"A … A … Abby … Abigail Grant," she replied nervously.

Lauren could see that Abby was overwhelmed so she tried to lighten the mood some.

"I take it you had no idea where you were headed tonight?" she asked laughingly.

"No, none at all."

"Sorry about that, but discretion is of the utmost importance. I'm sure you can understand."

Standing there still dazed and confused Abby said, "Who? What?"

"Dance with me," Lauren said reaching for Abby's arm, pulling her close.

Was there even music playing? If there was she couldn't hear it over the pounding of her heart as their bodies pressed together, remembering the warmth and the sweet scent of vanilla. "It was you," Abby said. This time however, the woman did not hide her face; instead, she gazed directly into Abby's eyes causing her to feel almost as if she were in a dream. Lauren's eyes were the most inviting shade of blue she had ever seen and she found herself unable to look away. It was as if Lauren had placed a spell on Abby and nothing else in the world mattered.

"Excuse me, Miss Lauren!"

"Not now, Alfred," she shouted back

"I'm terribly sorry, Miss Lauren, but Cook requested that I inform you that dinner is served and you know how she gets when you're late."

"Sorry, Alfred. We'll be right there."

"Listen. I know this is a lot for you to handle all at once, and you must have a million questions, so why don't you join me for dinner and I will explain as much as I can."

Abby simply nodded, unable to speak as Lauren reached for her hand and led her through a lavish maze of rooms toward the dining room where a very angry looking woman in chef's whites waited.

"I think we'd be more comfortable dining outside tonight," Lauren said to the angry woman.

"Certainly, Miss Lauren, right away," she replied as she scurried away waving her hands in the air and mumbling obscenities under her breath.

"Don't mind her, Abby. She's very cranky, but she's the best cook I've ever had."

She led Abby through the kitchen to what Abby assumed was the rear part of the house. They continued down a long narrow hall to a beautiful outdoor paradise surrounded by large rock formations, soft flowing waterfalls and an abundance of fragrant flowers.

They sat at a wrought iron table, which was barely big enough for the both of them. Their eyes met from across the table and Abby was again unable to look away from the crystal baby blues. Her heart began to race as Lauren's eyes darkened with desire. Abby swallowed hard as Lauren reached for her hand, gently stroking her finger over it. She was barely able to remain in her chair when Lauren leaned over the table and kissed her softly on the lips.

"Sorry. I just couldn't resist."

"It's okay," Abby replied nervously, wishing she'd been able to maintain her composure long enough to have kissed her back.

Suddenly, the cranky woman was back with a cart filled with food.

"I hope you're hungry! I wasn't sure what you liked so I had Cook prepare a few different choices." Abby nodded remembering again that she hadn't eaten since the night before.

"Thank-you, Cook. You can leave the cart and we'll help ourselves."

"Are you sure, Miss Lauren? It's no trouble."

"I'm sure, Cook," she replied giving her a look that suggested she wanted to be left alone.

"Perhaps your guest needs something?"

"I'm so sorry, Abby; I've been a terrible hostess. My mind has been on other things," She winked mischievously. "Is there anything that you would like? Anything at all?"

"No thank you, I'm fine"

"Very well then, I'll head to my room. Shall you want your breakfast in your room tomorrow, Miss Lauren?" she asked with a hint of disapproval.

Lauren once again captured Abby's eyes with her own and held them for a moment searching for the answer. Smiling, she replied, "Yes, I think that would be fine! Goodnight, Cook!"

"Goodnight, Miss Lauren."

"Sorry about that. She can be very difficult, but once you taste her cooking, you won't question my keeping her around."

"This looks wonderful!" Abby said shyly. There was an assortment of shrimp, steak, chicken, salads, vegetables, rice, fresh fruit and raspberry cheesecake.

"Help yourself," Lauren said as she poured them each a glass of wine.

Abby eagerly filled her plate with shrimp, steak and an assortment of freshly steamed vegetables, avoiding the chicken and rice as her mind drifted momentarily to her dinner with Erin the previous evening.

As they both settled into their chairs, plates full, Abby couldn't quite believe where she was and what she was doing. *This woman is a goddess! What in the world, does she want with me?*

"So, Abby, I guess you're wondering what this is all about."

"Yeah! I mean two hours ago, I was sitting alone in my hotel room and now I'm having dinner with Lauren Waters of all people. I guess it'd be silly to tell you now that I've always been a big fan of your work."

"Well, that's good, I'm not sure I'd have been able to get you into bed tonight if you hadn't been a fan."

Abby swallowed awkwardly and nearly chocked on a bite of steak. Suddenly, very nervous again, she quickly downed the rest of her wine.

Lauren smiled as she refilled Abby's glass. "Relax okay!" Lauren said as she reached across the table to touch Abby's hand sending shivers through her body.

"I'm just a person, no different than you. And I don't bite, unless that's what you like, of course?"

Abby nervously dropped her fork, causing a loud clanging sound as it landed on her plate.

"Sorry!"

"Relax already! Don't make me come back across this table!" she said jokingly, trying to lighten the mood.

Sensing Abby's continuing discomfort, she started to tell the story of how Abby ended up there. "I've been single for about a month now. Far too long for me. I went to ED's Wednesday night in search of a new girlfriend. I was there the whole night, admiring you from a corner table. Aside from the obvious physical attraction, I was awed by the fact that you were actually able to make Erin smile. She hasn't done that in months. Then I watched you with the little blonde. You seduced her so easily I knew for sure you were the one."

# Chapter Five

"The one?" Abby questioned.

"Yes, the one I've chosen to be my new girlfriend."

Abby gasped in shock. Who the hell did she think she was? "I don't do girlfriends and we don't even know each other," she said angrily.

"You will agree, I am sure of it," Lauren challenged.

"No ... No, I won't," Abby said as she started to stand up.

"Abby!" Lauren implored, grabbing her arm. "Just give me a chance. Give me tonight. Then you can decide, but I know you're the one."

Their eyes met again, and although she tried to fight it, she could not help her attraction to Lauren.

"Please Abby!" she pleaded again "You know you want to say yes! It's written all over your face."

"No, I can't do this." Abby said trying to convince herself as much as Lauren "I can't ..."

She was suddenly unable to speak as Lauren's lips met hers. Abby willed herself to pull away, but she was physically unable to resist the soft, sensuous woman. Lauren would not take no for an answer as she pushed the still resisting Abby against the back wall of the waterfall so forcefully it nearly knocked the breath out of both of them. She forced her tongue between Abby's lips as the water poured down over them.

Abby knew she was stronger than this, both physically and emotionally, but she was either unable or unwilling to fight it anymore as she relaxed, taking Lauren's tongue into her mouth, allowing it to dance with hers. She felt faint, overwhelmed with passion and desire.

Lauren cupped Abby's breast gently stroking her nipple with her thumb. When Abby moaned in response, Lauren squeezed her nipple so hard that she nearly cried out in pain. Moments later, a deep yearning between her legs eclipsed the pain and Abby held Lauren to her breast, encouraging her to continue.

"Fuck me."

"Say please."

"Please fuck me!"

Lauren reached between them, unzipped Abby's jeans without difficulty and quickly lowered them to the ground. Her blue eyes were nearly black now with desire as she locked eyes with Abby and abruptly plunged three of her long, slender fingers into Abby. Abby's eyes slammed shut in pain and exhilaration. Lauren remained perfectly still except for the beating of her heart until Abby opened her eyes, begging for more. With that, Lauren repeatedly thrust into Abby's wetness until she felt Abby's body stiffen and then collapse into her arms.

"Now that I have your attention. Do we have an understanding?" Lauren asked.

Abby again could do no more than nod agreeably.

"Good! Let's get you warmed up in a hot shower and into some dry clothes," she said as she led Abby to the pool house.

"Shout if you need anything, I'm going to find some dry clothes, but I'll be right back," Lauren said as she left Abby to her thoughts, picked up the wet clothes, and ran into the house to change.

Abby sat for a few minutes overwhelmed, still unable to form a coherent thought in her mind. *Congratulations Abigail, it would appear as though you've had your first orgasm,* she thought to herself as she struggled to her feet and stepped into the shower. Rarely did she let the women she slept with touch her, and never, had she let one of them bring her to orgasm. It was another one of the rules she followed to remain distant.

Lauren quickly showered and changed into a silky short set and a robe. She smiled at her reflection in the mirror, proud of herself for not letting Abby get away. She headed back to the patio stopping briefly at Alfred's door on the way by.

"Alfred?" she called as she knocked. "Do you have that information I requested?"

"Yes, Miss Lauren, please come in."

"No surprises?" she asked.

"No, Miss Lauren. Miss Abigail checks out just fine. Nothing unusual," he said as he handed her an envelope.

"Thank you, Alfred. Could you ask Russell to go to the Hyatt tomorrow and gather Abby's belongings and take care of her expenses?"

"Surely, Miss Lauren. I presume Miss Abigail will be staying then?" he questioned.

"Yes, Alfred, I think she will."

"Very well then. Goodnight, Miss Lauren."

"Goodnight, Alfred," she said before closing the door and returning to the patio

Abby had still not returned so Lauren cleared their dinner plates replacing them each with a piece of raspberry cheesecake. She refilled their wine glasses, settled into her chair and began reading the report Alfred had given her.

Abigail Carson Grant *Carson?*
DOB July 9, 1981
1621 Redwood Lane, Lansing, Michigan

"Hey, are you okay?" Lauren asked as Abby finally made her way from the pool house dressed in a warm thick robe. Her still-wet hair slicked back. "A few more minutes and I would have gone in to check on you."

"I'm okay, really. Better than okay." Abby smiled shyly, amazed that this soft, sweet, gentle woman was the same woman who had ravaged her body so violently only a few minutes earlier.

"I'm sorry about earlier. I don't usually ... I mean, are you sure you're okay?"

"Yeah, I'm sure," Abby said before joining Lauren at the table. "What are you reading?

"It's your security clearance. I hope you're not mad, but I can't be too careful. Crazy stalker types out there you know?"

"I understand, but wouldn't it have been more prudent to have that information earlier?"

"I suppose so, but I wasn't worried," she replied. "Carson?"

"My Dad wanted a boy to carry on his name. Unfortunately he got a girl and I got Carson."

"Degree in engineering from MSU," Lauren read out loud, as she continued to browse through Abby's file.

"If you have any questions you could just ask me you know," Abby said nervously as she watched Lauren read, not sure which of her deep dark secrets were about to be exposed.

"I know, but what would be the fun in that. I like to watch you squirm. Now eat your cheesecake; you must be famished."

Abby ate her cheesecake and watched Lauren as she read through the endless pages of information no doubt divulging the most intimate details of Abby's life. Abby's heart began to pound in her chest as she admired Lauren's hands, remembering what they had done to her just moments earlier.

"Sorry for the interruption, but I have to take this," Lauren said as she reached for her now ringing cell phone.

"Yes, Karen."

"No, I can't do that."

"No."

"You tell them that the earliest I can be there is Thursday, I'm busy until then."

"I don't care."

"I waited there all last week for them to do retakes and they didn't get around to it. Now I'm on vacation until Thursday," she said as she slammed the phone closed.

"Sorry about that. They wanted me to fly back to Australia tomorrow to finish doing retakes on my latest movie."

"No problem. I understand, but what's so important here that you can't leave until Thursday?"

"Normally, I would just have gone, but you and I have only just begun to get to know one another and since you don't fly out until Wednesday, I thought we could spend that time together."

"You're messing with your career here, Lauren, and I haven't agreed to anything beyond tonight so why would you do that?"

"Maybe so, but I have a feeling you'll be sticking around," she said as she flashed those crystal blue eyes at Abby.

Her breath caught and she was suddenly captivated once again by Lauren's kisses. Soft and gentle this time. Not hurried. "Why can't I seem to say no to you?" she asked as she melted into Lauren's arms. Their tongues danced in perfect rhythm as their hands searched for what they desired. Their bodies swaying in perfect unison.

"Let's go to bed, sweetheart," Lauren whispered, taking Abby by the hand and leading her up the three flights of stairs to her lavish bedroom.

Navy coloured satin sheets adorned the king sized bed. An amazing nearly life-size painting of two womanly figures embracing covered one wall adjacent to the French doors leading out to the small balcony overlooking the patio. Lauren cracked open the French doors to allow the sounds of the waterfalls and the scents of the citrus trees to permeate the room.

"Come here," Lauren said dropping her robe and short set to the floor.

Abby approached slowly taking in the sight of the beautiful Lauren Waters, desire overriding any thoughts of good sense and reason she may have had left. Lauren reached for Abby's belt, gently untying her robe, allowing her hands to explore the tender skin beneath it for a moment before sliding it off her shoulders and allowing it to fall to the floor next to her own.

"I've never wanted anyone as much as I want you right now," she said as she pulled Abby's face to hers, their lips meeting with urgency.

Abby led Lauren over to the bed resting her full weight on top of her. "So, Miss Waters, what is your pleasure?" Abby asked teasingly.

"My pleasure," Lauren responded by flipping them over in one swift motion, "will be to hear you scream out my name."

Abby once again realized that she was not in control of this situation and she wondered if she ever would be.

Lauren began teasing Abby's nipples with the flicker of her tongue, enjoying the satisfaction of them swelling and hardening in response to her touch. As she continued to caress her breasts, she spread Abby's legs with her narrow hips feeling the wetness against her skin. Abby was certain she had never been this excited. Never before had she needed this so badly.

"Please hurry," Abby urged, pushing Lauren's hand down between them to meet her throbbing center.

"I want to taste you," Lauren replied as she left Abby's swollen nipple moving down Abby's body pushing her own breast against Abby's wetness spreading her legs further apart with her shoulders.

"God, Lauren, please hurry," Abby pleaded.

Lauren used her expert tongue to tease Abby gently, sending her body into rhythmic waves of pleasure. "Lauren, please I can't take it anymore."

"Yes Lauren, Yes, Yes, Yesss!" Abby screamed when Lauren plunged two fingers inside her while sucking on her clit. Consumed by pleasure, Abby wrapped her legs around Lauren's shoulders and pulled herself harder into Lauren's mouth, desperately seeking release. Letting herself go, her body rising and falling as waves of her orgasm took over her body. Unable to stop, it went on and on until at last her body fell limply on the bed. Exhausted, trembling, unable to move or speak, Abby lie there unsure if she was awake or if she had just dreamt the last half hour of her life. Lauren looked up and smiled, waiting for her to release her fingers.

"You okay, sweetheart?"

Abby could only nod. She was unable to form words.

Once Abby relaxed and finally released her fingers, Lauren gently moved up to hold Abby in her arms, gently kissing her and urging her to go to sleep. Abby could not help but agree. Her body was spent and lifeless. She could not have pleased Lauren if she tried since her whole body felt like a bowl of Jell-O.

"Sorry," she said as she drifted off into sleep in Lauren's arms.

Abby opened her eyes and looked around the room. For a few minutes, she felt disoriented in her unfamiliar surroundings. She rolled over sensing someone else in the bed with her and was disappointed to see Lauren. Suddenly the memories of what she had done the night before flooded back to her. She had so many regrets. She should never have let this happen. The only reason she had agreed to any of this was to get Erin out of her mind and that hadn't worked. Dreams of the beautiful bar owner, frequently interrupted her otherwise peaceful sleep. Waking up next to Lauren paled in comparison to waking up next to Erin. Although she didn't understand her feelings for Erin, she knew she didn't feel anything for Lauren.

"Good morning," Lauren said sitting next to Abby reading a book.

"What time is it?" Abby asked sleepily.

"It's nearly nine. How are you feeling this morning?"

Abby smiled. Despite her regrets, she did have a good time the night before. "I'm good. Great in fact, but I really need a shower."

"Okay, while you do that, I'll have Cook bring up breakfast and we can eat out on the balcony. I though maybe we could go out today. Catch the art fair or something?"

Abby sat up nearly panic stricken. Not only had she spent the night, but now, Lauren was making plans for later. "Let me just go take a shower and we can talk about it after," Abby said hurrying to the bathroom.

She just sat on the shower floor letting the water poor over her as she replayed the last twenty-four hours in her mind repeatedly. *You can do this Abby,* she reasoned with herself. *You had a great time last night and millions of other women around the world would die to be the object of Lauren Waters' desire, but you promised yourself you would never put yourself in a position to get hurt. Just follow the rules and you won't get hurt! But you've already broken several of them. Maybe it's time to take a chance. Just get through this weekend and you can go back to your life. It's simple, just don't get emotionally involved and everything will be fine. You did want someone to show you around town after all.*

"Abby, are you okay in there?" Lauren interrupted her thoughts.

"Yeah! I'll be out in a minute!" Abby shouted as she quickly finished her shower.

"Feel better?" Lauren asked as Abby approached the table a few minutes later.

"Much. Thank you."

"You must be starving? You didn't eat much last night?"

"Yeah! I could definitely eat," she replied, helping herself to bacon, eggs and French toast.

"Miss Lauren! Sorry to interrupt, but Miss Abigail's things are here. Where would you like them?" a voice on the intercom said.

"My things?"

"Alfred, why don't you just send them up?"

"Yes, Miss Lauren. Right away."

"My things?" Abby protested again.

"Okay, relax. I thought you might decide to stay so I took the liberty of checking you out of your hotel and sending for your things. If that's not okay, we can take you back. It's no big deal."

"No big deal! No big deal! *You* decided that I wanted to stay. Well, let's get something straight right now. I decide what I do, not you. I'm not sure how things work in your world, but in my world, I'm in charge."

"Abby, calm down! I didn't mean to imply anything. I just thought we were getting along so well that it would be easier if you just stayed here. Abby, I really like you. I really do, and I'd like for you to stay, but if you want to leave, I'll understand."

"You don't even know me. Except for what's in that file you're still reading, you know nothing about me," Abby challenged.

"I'd like to get to know you better. Just give me a chance," Lauren pleaded. "Just a minute," Lauren yelled as she got up to answer the door.

"Here are Miss Abigail's things, and her clothes from last night. Did you need anything else at the moment?"

"Thank you Alfred, we're fine for now."

"Very well then," Alfred said as he closed the door behind him.

"Abby? I'm very sorry if I upset you. That was not my intention," Lauren said smiling, meeting Abby's angry eyes.

"Don't look at me!" Abby said angrily.

"Why?"

"Because you make it impossible to say no to you," she shouted, meeting Lauren's blue eyes trying her best to remain angry.

"Are you sure it's my eyes, or is it maybe that what you really want to say is yes, Abby?" she said, leaning forward to kiss Abby's lips. Abby shuddered and her heart began to pound against her chest. *How does she do this to you Abby?*

"So, you'll stay then?" Lauren said pulling away.

"Yes."

"Good, now let's finish breakfast so we can try to beat some of the crowds."

"Um! None of my clothes are clean; I was supposed to do laundry today."

"The clothes you had on last night are clean. They're on the bed and if you give me the rest of your clothes I'll send them down to be washed."

Abby finished her breakfast and got dressed while Lauren showered. As she piled her dirty clothes on the floor, checking to make sure her pockets were empty, she came across the shirt she had worn to Erin's. She again brought it close to her face, inhaling deeply, feeling comforted by Erin's lingering scent. She debated over washing it. *Maybe next time*, she decided as she put the unwashed shirt back into her suitcase.

Lauren entered the room dressed in a pair of khaki shorts, a skin-tight black top and a pair of sandals. Her hair was pulled back in a ponytail through her black ball cap.

"Are these all the clothes you have?"

"Yeah."

"I'll have Alfred take care of them for you. Didn't you bring any shorts?"

"No, I hadn't planned on being outside much during the day so I didn't bring any."

"Okay then, we'll stop on the way back and get you some. Are you ready?"

"Yeah, I guess so. Aren't you worried about being recognized?"

"Not with my sunglasses on and besides, even if someone did recognize me at the art fair it wouldn't be a big deal."

"Okay," Abby replied, before following Lauren through the house to the front door. "When we get back will you show me the rest of the house, please?"

"I intend to give you a very *special* tour!" Lauren replied, smiling seductively.

They rode in near silence as they each took the time to process the events of last night and this morning.

"This is as close as I can get without drawing a crowd, Miss Lauren," Russell said.

"Okay, Russell."

"Do you have your beeper, Miss Lauren?"

"Yes, Russell," Lauren answered slightly annoyed.

"I'll meet you at the front gate if there's a problem."

"Okay. We should be out in a couple of hours and I do not expect any trouble today," Lauren said as they got out of the car and headed toward the entrance.

"He's very protective of you," Abby noted

"He is. He's been with me forever and he knows how to handle any situation that comes up," Lauren replied as she handed the man at the gate the twenty-dollar entry fee.

"You don't have to pay my way you know! I do have my own money."

"I know that. It's in your file. But I asked you to join me today so it's my treat okay?"

"Fair enough."

They spent the next two and a half hours just walking through the exhibits hand in hand talking about the various pieces that they found interesting. Abby found herself wondering what certain pieces might look like hung in Erin's loft. She knew being with Lauren was a mistake. She should have booked a seat on the first flight home after leaving Erin's that morning. The longer she stayed here the more complicated things were going to get.

# Chapter Six

"Russell, we need to stop at the mall for a minute on the way home."

"Yes, Miss Lauren."

They rode to the mall in silence. Abby trying to understand how much her life had changed in just a few days.

"East entrance please, Russell," Lauren said as they pulled into the mall parking lot.

"I'll wait right here," Russell said as he opened the door to let them out.

"I know the perfect store," Lauren exclaimed as she led the way through the mall trying to avoid large groups of people.

As soon as they walked into the store, Lauren began picking out clothes for Abby to try on. Abby wasn't sure if Lauren was being controlling again, or if she was just in a hurry, so she let her continue. "Here, go try these on, I'll look for some more," Lauren said while handing Abby five pairs of shorts and pointing to the fitting rooms at the back of the store.

Abby began trying on pair after pair and was surprised that each pair looked very good on her. Lauren definitely had an eye for fashion.

"How's it going?" Lauren asked as she stood outside the fitting room door with a few more pairs of shorts.

"Good, everything fits," Abby replied.

"Open the door so I can see."

Abby opened the door and took the remaining shorts from Lauren. "Those are cute," Lauren noted, looking at the shorts Abby was wearing. "Turn around so I can see the back." As Abby turned around, Lauren gently but firmly pushed her up against the wall and closed the door behind her. "What are you doing?" Abby scolded her.

"You're not going to cause a scene, are you, sweetheart?" she said kissing her neck and gently reaching around to stroke Abby's nipples which hardened immediately.

"No," Abby replied trying to catch her breath.

"I didn't think so," Lauren teased as she reached between Abby's thighs gently stroking her. Abby was having a difficult time standing up so she balanced herself against the wall with her hands. "I think these are my favourite," Lauren said pulling the now soaked shorts down to the floor. She quickly returned her hand to Abby's wet center stroking her tenderly. "Come for me Abby," she said just as Abby's body stiffened and her orgasm took hold of her. Lauren placed her free hand over Abby's mouth to stifle her scream until her body relaxed. Smiling, Lauren stood there holding Abby for a moment before walking out. "I'll be waiting in the car."

"Damn you, Lauren Waters!" Abby said under her breath trying to regain her composure. She quickly got dressed fearing a salesperson would soon be checking on her since she'd been in there so long. She chose three pairs of shorts and brought them to the cashier ripping the tag off the pair she'd just had on so the cashier would not notice the wet spot.

"Did you get everything you needed today," the cashier asked as she totalled the purchase.

"Yes," Abby replied blushing slightly, hoping they hadn't seen Lauren join her in the room.

"Thank you, have a great day," she said as Abby rushed out of the store and headed back to the car.

She arrived to find Lauren sitting in the car waiting for her, smiling mischievously. "What took you so long?"

Abby did not answer as she sat down avoiding Lauren's charming smile. She stared out the window wondering what she had gotten herself into with this woman. She was definitely never boring, but Abby needed to be in control, and so far, she had been unable to gain it even for a moment.

"Are you going to pout all the way back?"

Abby nodded without looking away from the window.

"Good, you're very cute when you pout," Lauren replied.

*Damn you, Lauren Waters*, she thought to herself again, not giving in to her urge to smile.

"Shit, not today!" Lauren exclaimed as they pulled into the driveway noticing Karen's car there.

"What?" Abby asked.

"My agent's here, I guess she didn't like being hung up on last night."

"Where the hell have you been?" Karen asked as they walked through the front door.

"Nice to see you, too," Lauren said sarcastically, walking past her.

"Don't you answer your phone anymore?"

"No, I've decided not to," Lauren replied sharply.

"And who the hell is this now?" Karen said accusingly.

"Sorry, Abby this is Karen, Karen this is Abby."

"Nice to meet you, Karen," Abby said politely, extending her hand to Karen who did not return the gesture.

"Whatever. Will you go do something while I talk some sense into Lauren?" she said dismissively.

"Lauren, I'm going to go take a shower okay."

"I think that's a good idea, sweetheart, then, if you want, you can ask Cook to make you something to eat, I'll probably be quite a while. I'm sorry," she said giving Abby a long soft kiss before she took Karen into the library.

Abby could hear them arguing as she walked away wondering why Karen had been so rude to her. She enjoyed the time alone while she took a long hot shower and put on some clean clothes. It had been an intense couple of days and she was glad for the break.

She headed down to the kitchen and shyly looked around for Cook who she found sitting in a corner of the kitchen watching some program on a small black and white television.

"Cook?" Abby called fearfully.

"Yes! Um Yes. Is there something you need, Madam?" she said as she quickly turned off the television and scurried over to her.

"Lauren is busy with Karen so she suggested I see you about dinner. I'd be happy to make my own, but I wasn't sure you'd be pleased to find me rummaging through your kitchen."

"You are very thoughtful, Madam, not at all like the others. I'd be happy to make you some dinner, now tell me, what would you like?"

"My name is Abby; I guess we've not been properly introduced. What did you mean by the others?"

"Oh! Nothing really. I spoke out of turn, Miss Abby, I'm sorry."

"Okay then," Abby said making a mental note of her slip up. "Could I help you prepare dinner, I've nothing better to do for the time being?"

"Oh my! You really are something aren't you; no wonder Miss Lauren fancies you so. I'd be happy to share my kitchen with you this evening provided you don't tell anyone."

"Deal!" Abby replied as they walked back into the kitchen together.

For the next few hours, they had a wonderful time. While they prepared dinner, they talked easily, discussing anything and everything except for Lauren. Even though Abby had questions, it would have been inappropriate for Cook to answer them. Cook seemed to enjoy herself as well, even taking the time to sit with Abby while she ate dinner.

"Can I get you anything else?" Cook asked.

"No thank you, that was fabulous."

"Very well then. Goodnight, Miss Abby."

"Goodnight, Cook."

"Miss Abby?"

"Yes."

"Feel free to rummage around the kitchen anytime you please."

"Thank you, Cook," she said as she walked away. She smiled to herself, having won over this very difficult woman. Abby decided to go check on Lauren, but wasn't really surprised to hear them still arguing as she approached the door. There was clearly more to Lauren and Karen's relationship than she was aware of, but she wouldn't get any answers by eavesdropping, so, she decided to go upstairs, curl up in bed and watch television.

"Hey Erin"

"Hey Frankie!" Erin said as she picked up her apron and got ready to start her shift.

"You okay?" Frankie asked.

"Um hum," Erin nodded.

"Dinah again?"

"No, not this time."

"How was your date the other night?"

"Not as planned," Erin replied sharply.

With that, Frankie knew not to press anymore. She had learned over the years that when Erin was ready to talk, she would. "I think it's going to be busy tonight. Most spring breakers will be out enjoying their last night in town."

"I hope so, last night was busy, but still too much time to think," Erin replied, remembering how often she had looked up to see who was walking through the door. Her heart refused to listen to her mind telling her that Abby would never again walk through that door.

"Oh! Erin, I wish there was something I could do or say to make you feel better. If I wasn't straight, I'd marry you and we'd live happily ever after," Frankie joked.

"I know, you tell me that all the time. Thank you for being who you are. You have no idea what your friendship means to me," she said while giving Frankie a gentle hug.

She had hired Frankie five years ago to help her manage the weekend crowds and she had been an invaluable friend and employee ever since. The fact that Frankie was straight and married did little to discourage the countless women who found her charming and attractive. She was good for business, Erin reminded herself while surrendering to the guilty pleasure of admiring Frankie's long slender legs and beautiful long blond hair. She never failed to wear a tight t-shirt which hugged her beautiful double D's. More than just her sheer beauty, Frankie's personality was her best asset. She was very personable and over the years had become very good at turning down the advances of the hundreds of women who repeatedly made passes at her. She never got flustered; in fact, she was rewarded very well for her efforts when she occasionally, danced for them seductively on the bar. Erin was very glad to have Frankie in her life.

It was a busy night and a line formed outside the club. Every year it seemed to get busier especially around spring break. Erin had always been conflicted about this because she had purposely located off the beaten path and had avoided all forms of advertising so the locals and celebrities would feel comfortable without all the tourists. Every year she had re-evaluated the volumes of tourists and considered moving to a different location until the crowds again became too overwhelming. Perhaps this would be the year. The change would probably do her good.

They worked feverishly, Erin thankful for the distraction of the endless stream of women making their way to and from the bar.

"Hi," Tiffany said. "Could I have a Bud Light please?"

"Sure thing, sweetie," Erin replied and smiled when she recognized Tiffany as the girl Abby seduced the other night.

"Thanks," Tiffany replied when Erin handed her the beer. "Um ... I don't suppose you've seen the woman I was talking to here at the bar the other night. She was supposed to meet me here so I ditched my friends. I tried to call her, but they said she had already checked out."

"No, I haven't seen her here yet. Where was she staying?" Erin asked curiously, not sure Tiffany would answer and not quite sure why that information would be useful to her.

"The Hyatt," Tiffany replied. "If you see her, please tell her I'm looking for her."

"Will do," Erin replied sympathetically.

The rest of the evening seemed to drag on endlessly. Erin waited anxiously for Abby to walk through the door, but she never did.

"Last call!" Frankie yelled.

The club emptied quickly after that as everyone headed to after hours locations. While Erin finished drying the last of the bar glasses she noticed Tiffany still sitting at one of the tables.

"Hey! She didn't show huh?" she asked, meeting the young woman's eyes. She was very pretty Erin thought. If nothing else, Abby sure knew how to pick them. "Sorry!"

"It's okay. I wasn't sure she would, but she sounded excited about it yesterday."

Erin sat down handing the young woman another beer, "It's on me."

"Thanks."

"Maybe something came up and she had to go home unexpectedly?" she said trying to console Tiffany.

"Yeah, that's probably what happened. I just don't know what I'm going to do now?"

"About what?"

"My friends all took off for the night and I wasn't supposed to meet up with them until tomorrow," she said pathetically.

"What's your name sweetie?" Erin asked even though she knew the answer.

"Tiffany. What's yours?" she replied

"My name is Erin and I'd be happy to let you sleep on the couch upstairs if you want."

"Really?" Tiffany replied excitedly.

"Sure it's no problem, just let me lock up okay?"

"Okay," Tiffany replied as she finished her beer and waited for Erin to lock up.

Erin quickly locked the doors and turned off the lights, suddenly feeling a little better. At least she'd have some company tonight. "Okay, Tiffany, follow me," she said as she led her upstairs to the loft.

"Can I get you a drink or something?" Erin offered.

"No thanks, I think I've had enough," she said, smiling, as she looked deeply into Erin's eyes. "Erin?" she said reaching for her hands, "I really would rather not sleep out here alone on the couch."

Erin pulled away, "What are you suggesting?"

"I'm suggesting, this," she said as she pulled Erin close to her kissing her hard on the lips.

"I don't think so," Erin replied, pulling away from Tiffany in shock. Less than an hour ago, she had been nearly inconsolable about Abby and now she wanted to share Erin's bed. How fickle, she thought to herself?

"Don't you think I'm attractive?" Tiffany asked.

Erin caught Tiffany's eyes and held them as she wrestled with the guilt and her desire to satisfy her own needs. *Oh, what the hell* she thought to herself, Tiffany would be leaving town tomorrow and perhaps the distraction would be good for her.

She pulled Tiffany close to her, their bodies now touching, the need they both shared drawing them even closer together. "You're beautiful," Erin whispered before capturing Tiffany's lips with her own, softly at first, gently running her fingers through Tiffany's long blond hair, pulling her closer, feeling the heat of her body as any bit of good sense she had remaining was quickly washed away, replaced with nothing but need.

Without warning, Tiffany became hurried, feverishly pulling at Erin's clothes, her hands just grasping at anything she could get a hold of.

"Stop!" Erin said as she reached for Tiffany's hands and held them still. "What's your hurry?" she asked, still holding onto Tiffany's hands. "If we're going to do this, we're going to do it my way?"

"I'm sorry!" Tiffany said unsure of what she had done wrong. "Most women just want me to …"

Erin interrupted her. "I am not most women," Erin said releasing her hands and gently lifting her chin to meet her eyes then kissing her softly on the lips. They stood for several minutes just holding each other, their kisses soft and slow.

"This is nice," Tiffany said, breaking away for a moment.

"Yes, it is," Erin replied before taking Tiffany's hand and leading her to the bedroom.

As they stood at the edge of the bed, Erin slowly, but methodically, kissed Tiffany, while her hands delicately explored her body. She gently guided Tiffany back onto the bed and laid her full weight on top of her. She kissed her softly on the lips before gently dragging her lower lip over Tiffany's cheek, then softly kissing her closed eyelids trailing light kisses down to her ear before whispering again, "You are so beautiful."

Tiffany moaned as Erin gently cupped her breasts and lightly stroked her nipples with her index finger causing them to swell and harden with delight. Wanting, needing to feel skin on skin, flesh on flesh, woman on woman, Erin pulled back removing her own shirt and bra, revealing herself to the beautiful woman lying beneath her. She gently pulled Tiffany up to meet her and kissed her passionately wanting to feel her body against her own. She slowly pulled Tiffany's sweater off and began to kiss her neck as she released the clasp of her bra with one hand. She gasped as she slid the bra from Tiffany's shoulders exposing her beautiful voluptuous breasts. She spent a moment just gazing at their beauty before laying Tiffany back down on the bed. She moaned softly as breast met breast and lips met lips once again.

Erin began slowly trailing wet kisses down Tiffany's neck and chest, joining her hands, which had already made their way to the voluptuous mounds. Her tongue traced circles around Tiffany's hard nipples causing her to moan. As Tiffany tried to push Erin harder to her breast, Erin quickly moved away from her breast back to her mouth kissing her deeply before finally moving back down to take one of her nipples into her mouth, holding it there while her tongue danced around, over it, for a few moments before moving to the other one.

Feeling Tiffany's body undulating beneath her, her breathing rapid and shallow she decided to slow things down again by moving back up to her mouth. Tiffany whimpered as she left her breast, but the whimpers were quickly silenced as Erin began kissing her very softly and slowly again, running her fingers through her hair, caressing her beautiful face with her hands.

When Tiffany's breathing returned to a normal rhythm, Erin made her way back down, trailing wet kisses over her chest, pausing briefly at each breast before continuing down her flat stomach. She took her time making sure to kiss every inch of her stomach before teasingly running her tongue across Tiffany's waistline and using her teeth to unbutton her jeans.

"Let's get these out of the way," she teased, slowly removing Tiffany's jeans and then her own.

She lay back down on top of Tiffany, whose hips had risen to meet her thigh. Feeling the wet heat against her skin made Erin moan in anticipation. She reached down to feel the waiting wetness as Tiffany began to raise her hips urgently to meet Erin's hand. Not ready for this moment to end just yet, Erin pulled her hand away and slowed the pace down again, despite Tiffany's pleading. After several moments, she decided to put an end to this torture. As she once again began her slow decent, Erin kissed and caressed every inch of Tiffany's body all the while looking into her desperate eyes. She smiled before she plunged her tongue into her wetness, eagerly drinking up the sweet nectar. Feeling Tiffany's orgasm looming, Erin used her free hand to pleasure herself,

Unable to move, as their bodies recovered, they could do no more than look into each other's eyes until Tiffany was finally able to reach down and pull Erin toward her.

"That was … Um Wow!" I didn't think it could be that good," Tiffany said kissing Erin softly.

"Then you're sleeping with the wrong women," Erin joked.

"What can I do to please you?" Tiffany asked running a finger over Erin's nipple.

Erin quickly grabbed her hand and stopped her. "Just relax," she said wrapping her arms around her.

"Are you sure? Is there something wrong?"

"No, nothing's wrong, just relax okay!"

"Okay," she said, finally relaxing into Erin's arms.

Erin was happy. It had been a long time since she'd pleased a woman like this. Even with Dinah, the last year or so, sex had been infrequent and when it did happen, it was fast and impersonal. She should have known back then that there was something going on.

As happy as she was this very moment, she could not help but wonder what this night might have been like had it been Abby in her bed. She thought of how good it felt to be in Abby's arms as she drifted off into a peaceful sleep.

Erin woke to the sound of the shower running remembering with a smile the look on Tiffany' s face as wave after wave of her orgasm washed through her body.

"Morning, Erin," she said, when she emerged from the bathroom dressed and ready to leave. "I didn't want to wake you, you looked so peaceful, but I have to get going."

"Thanks, I had a good sleep for a change. Are you sure you can't stay for a while?"

"I wish I could, but I have a cab waiting downstairs. Thank you so much for last night. I'll never forget it," she said as she kissed Erin on the cheek and left.

# Chapter Seven

Abby woke to the sound of a ringing cell phone. "Will you answer that for me, Abby?" Lauren yelled from the bathroom.

"Hello," Abby said flipping open the phone.

"Who's this?" an angry voice asked.

"This is Abby, who are you?" Abby countered.

"What are you doing answering Lauren's phone and what the hell are you still doing there. I told her to get rid of you."

"Karen! I should have recognized the bitterness in your voice. Lauren is in the shower. I'll tell her you called," Abby said before slamming the phone shut. *What a bitch!*

"Hey," Lauren said when she appeared from the bathroom, dressed in a skirt and heels. She wore a beautiful ruffled blouse and her hair was down. "Who was on the phone?"

"Karen," Abby replied dejectedly.

"Ouch, sorry!" Lauren said sympathetically as she leaned down to kiss Abby on the forehead. "Something's come up and I have to go out for a couple of hours. Feel free to wander around or ask Alfred for the keys to my car if you want to go somewhere. I shouldn't be too late and I'll explain everything when I get back, but right now, I really need to go before Karen calls again to yell at me for being late," she said before grabbing her cell phone and heading out the door.

What an interesting morning it had been so far, Abby thought to herself, crawling out of bed to take a shower. She wondered if Lauren had even come to bed at all last night. She certainly didn't make a sound if she did. Abby noted the stress on Lauren's face this morning and wondered what could have come up so quickly, that she had to leave in such a hurry? What was the deal with Karen anyway? Abby decided it was time to ask Cook a few questions. There was definitely more going on between Lauren and Karen than what Lauren had let on.

"Morning, Cook," she said as she poked her head into the kitchen.

"Miss Abby, come sit down, I have breakfast ready for you. Will Miss Lauren be joining you?"

"No, she had to leave unexpectedly this morning. Something to do with Karen."

"That menace, I cannot wait until the day I won't have to deal with her anymore."

Abby looked at her questioningly as she took a seat at the table.

"It's really not for me to tell you, Miss Abby, but I think you're a lovely person and, as long as you promise not to say anything, I'll give you some of the details."

"I promise," Abby replied as she began to eat her breakfast.

"Well, I wasn't around back then, but Miss Lauren first met her about five years ago. She had been looking for a new agent, and Miss Karen came highly recommended. She was very aggressive and did wonders for Miss Lauren's career."

"Go on," Abby encouraged.

"Things were fine for a couple of years until Miss Lauren became very successful. She had won an Oscar and bought this house and she had a beautiful girlfriend whom she had been with for a while."

"So what happened?"

"Miss Karen became very jealous; she wanted Miss Lauren for herself. Well, really, she wanted what Miss Lauren had. She found a way to interfere with their relationship and caused a break-up. Miss Lauren was heartbroken, and you'll never guess who was there to pick up the pieces? Miss Karen manoeuvred her way right into Miss Lauren's bed. She moved in here and started taking charge, treating us all badly. They seemed happy for a little while, but soon, they fought terribly about everything. They would break up and get back together, break up and get back together. It was terrible, violent even. About a year ago, Miss Lauren had enough; she called it quits and told Miss Karen to leave for good. Miss Karen responded by threatening legal action if she did not continue to support her so Miss Lauren kept her on as her agent and paid her expenses. Since then, Miss Lauren has dated a few women, but none that really seemed to make her happy and Miss Karen continued to interfere and cause problems, she even paid one of them off. I think the longest any one of them stuck around was a month."

"Really?" Abby looked at her knowingly. "Anything else I should know?"

"No, I think I've already said too much," Cook replied.

"Don't worry, your secret's safe with me. And just so you know, Karen is already trying to get rid of me."

"Filthy wench!"

"Thanks for breakfast, it was wonderful. And thanks for being candid."

"You're welcome, Miss Abby. If you need anything at all, please let me know."

"I will," she said as she left the table and headed back upstairs to think.

She didn't want a relationship with Lauren or anybody else for that matter, but she despised people like Karen. She considered, for a moment, continuing this charade of a relationship with Lauren just to piss Karen off. That wouldn't be fair to Lauren though. Lauren wanted more from Abby than she was ever going to give her. She tried to be honest with Lauren from the beginning, but it was clear that she wasn't going to take no for an answer. When Lauren got back, Abby was going to sit her down and have a serious talk with her. They could have a couple of great days together and that was it. She was going to go home and never see Lauren again. Hopefully, she could leave the memories of Erin behind as well.

She decided to snoop around a bit in Lauren's room trying to get a better understanding of who the real person was behind all the glitz and glamour. She was shocked to find nothing. If Lauren had any secrets, she certainly wasn't hiding them in her bedroom. *The library*, she said to herself, remembering the desk in the library. It had looked as though that was where Lauren's real life was.

She headed for the library, mindful of the fact that Alfred might notice her going in there. She would tell him she was looking for a book to read out by the pool should he ask. She discreetly slipped past him, leaving the door open so as not to raise any suspicion and began by looking at all the pictures on the walls. Lauren had certainly met many influential people through the years. World leaders, successful business people, numerous other celebrities. Lauren's appearance in the pictures over the years spoke volumes about how she was feeling. In most of the early photos, Lauren was clearly happy, but over the years, she looked as if her spirit had been broken.

She glanced out the door to see if Alfred had been watching her and since he hadn't, she headed toward the desk. There wasn't an empty spot on the large oak desk, which was covered in papers, mostly scripts. Lauren's calendar was open and she noticed that she did not have a scheduled appointment this morning so she hadn't lied about it being unexpected. There was a large frame on the desk showing a recent picture of what appeared to be Lauren's family. Abby glanced out the door again quickly before opening the bottom drawer of the desk to find an old shoebox. "Aha!" she said as she pulled out the box, opened it, and found stacks of pictures.

They were pictures of Lauren with several different women. She found several of the same woman, who must have been the beautiful girlfriend Cook had mentioned. They looked like a very happy couple in the pictures. There was also a series of pictures of Lauren with Karen in which Lauren appeared to be small and fragile. Abby gasped when she found a picture of Lauren with Erin. They both looked so young it had to be nearly ten years ago. They made a beautiful couple. They complemented each other well. Erin must have known who Lauren was that night. Why hadn't she said anything? For some reason this bothered Abby, but she wasn't sure why.

There had to be at least twenty pictures of other women, but she didn't have time to look at them closely. The sound of Alfred stirring near the door caused her to panic and put the box away. She quickly stepped away from the desk and began to browse Lauren's vast book collection as Alfred appeared.

"Miss Abigail, is there something I can help you with?" he asked.

"No thanks, Alfred, I'm just looking for a book to read out by the pool."

"Wonderful, Miss Abigail, it's a beautiful day outside, it would be a shame to waste it indoors. Do call me if there is anything you need."

"I will, Alfred, thank you," she replied, quickly selecting a book and escaping upstairs hopeful that he had not noticed her rummaging through the desk.

She changed into a pair of shorts and a tank top and was preparing to leave the room, when she noticed her file sitting on the dresser. Deciding she needed to know what was in it, she took it with her, made her way down to the pool area, and made herself comfortable in a lounge chair.

The sun was hot, beating down on her skin, but there was a cool breeze blowing, just enough to make the temperature bearable. The sounds of the waterfalls in the distance made Abby blush slightly at the memory of her first night here. How had she let that happen so easily? *My how you've changed, Abigail.* She began to flip through the pages of the report not surprised to find all of her banking information. Certainly, Lauren would know that Abby wasn't with her for the money. She had managed to save up a hefty nest egg over the years. She continued through the report enjoying the information that was triggering memories from her childhood. Her mind drifted aimlessly back to her high school days, her first speeding ticket and once again to Mrs. Jones.

"Miss Abby!" Cook said as she approached Abby's chair. "I've made you some lunch, dear." She placed a plate of sandwiches and a pitcher of iced tea on the small table next to Abby's lounge chair.

Startled out of her fond memories, Abby quickly regained her composure and politely greeted the thoughtful woman. "Thank you, Cook, I was starving. Do you have time to join me?"

'I could spare a few minutes," Cook said, helping herself to one of the sandwiches.

"Have you heard from Lauren?" Abby asked. "It's nearly three o'clock, I was sure she'd be home by now."

"Sorry, Miss Abby, I have not heard from her, but please don't worry. Miss Lauren tends to go off on her own sometimes when she is trying to work things out. Russell is with her so I'm certain she is fine."

They basked silently in the sun for a few minutes before Cook headed back into the house. Not knowing what Lauren and Karen were arguing about last night was driving her crazy. She needed a distraction badly so she continued to read more of the report, stopping suddenly, when she read the name Helena Morris, formerly Helena Grant. The sight of her mother's name sent a shiver down her spine. She had long ago given up the thought of trying to make contact with her mother thinking that her mother knew where to find her if she ever felt the need to explain. She wondered how differently her life would have been had she had a mother to show her love and understanding.

She read on, noting that Helena lived only two hours from here. She was married and had two children, a boy, ten and a girl, five. She sure hadn't wasted much time after leaving them to start a new family.

She still longed for an explanation. It just didn't make sense the way she left so suddenly. Could she face her mother now after all these years? Maybe it was time, if nothing more than to get the answers she so desperately needed. Perhaps she could borrow Lauren's car tomorrow and pay Helena Morris a visit.

The sun was beginning to set now and Abby felt a bit of a chill setting in. It wasn't so much because of the cold, but because of the prospect of facing her mother after all these years. She changed her clothes and headed down to the kitchen to enjoy the meal that Cook had left for her in the warmer before heading out to her weekly wine-tasting meeting.

Lauren had arrived home around five o'clock, but she was still too upset to face Abby. She quietly snuck in the house and headed to her favourite room. The atrium was her sanctuary and no one ever bothered her there. The vaulted glass ceiling gave way to a spectacular view of the stars on a clear night. As she sat for a long time, replaying the events of the day she realized that she felt small and inconsequential. Karen had often made her feel that way. "Thank God it's over," she said to herself.

Karen obviously wasn't too happy about the settlement, but her lawyer had encouraged her to take it, or risk getting nothing at all, if it went to court. She reluctantly agreed. Karen had never hit her out in public before so she thought nothing of riding down in the elevator alone with her until she started her rant.

"You bitch!" Karen screamed. "You think you can just pay me and make me disappear?"

"Karen, calm down." Lauren sensed her rage building. Karen was on the verge of another one of her temper tantrums and she knew she was trapped in this elevator with her for a few more minutes.

"Calm down! Calm down …"

"You owe me, bitch!"

The right hook was new. Lauren had long ago learned to duck the left hook and had always been able to restrain Karen after the missed swing, but the right hook caught her totally off guard, catching her right under her left eye.

"Shit!" she said looking in the mirror at the pretty colours that were starting to appear under her left eye. It thankfully looked worse than it felt, or maybe, it was just that she was numb all over from the encounter.

It was nearly nine o'clock when Lauren finally made her way upstairs to her bedroom. She did not speak as she walked toward Abby, pulling her close, just wanting to feel Abby's body against her own. Abby saw the bruise under her left eye, but knew by the look on her face that this was not the time for questions or explanations. Lauren eyes were pleading for solace.

Tonight she was not the cool, confident Lauren that Abby had known. She appeared broken. Without speaking, Abby led Lauren to the bed, knowing that if she made love to Lauren tonight she would be giving more of herself than she had planned. She would be comforting her and comfort required emotion. Emotion required feeling and Abby did not want to develop feelings for Lauren.

Lauren did not protest as Abby undressed her and gently guided her down on the bed. She took her time, softly making love to Lauren; afraid she may break this fragile woman. The arrival of Lauren's orgasm brought only a few soft moans. It was as if, her body and mind were somehow disconnected. There was nothing sexual or romantic about the experience it was purely an emotional encounter. Abby, spent the rest of the night just holding her in her arms, willing her pain away, just as she had done a few nights ago with Erin.

When Erin finally woke is was nearly four o'clock. She knew she soon had to get ready for work, but she wanted to call the Hyatt just to make sure Abby had indeed checked out. She decided to call one of her old friends who worked at the hotel to see if he had any information.

"Hi Bobby, it's Erin!"

"Erin, honey! How are you? You sound much better than the last time I talked to you."

"Yeah, I'm doing a whole lot better."

"To what do I owe the honour of your call?"

"I was hoping for a favour?"

"Anything for you, honey."

"Could you tell me if Abigail Grant has checked out?"

"You know, I'm not supposed to tell you things like that."

"Please Bobby, I'll owe you forever."

"You already owe me forever. But, since you asked so nicely, not only did Ms. Grant check out, but her belongings were sent to 14321 Fox Run Drive this morning. Sounds like Miss Waters has found herself a new toy, if you know what I mean?"

"I was afraid of that. Thanks Bobby, stop by and see me soon. I miss you."

"Okay sweetie, I'll see you soon. Bye"

Damn.

"What the hell?" she shouted to herself as she stood in front of the mirror. At some point last night, Tiffany had left a huge hickey on her neck. That's going to require some sort of explanation, she thought to herself, smiling as she got in the shower and prepared for work.

A half hour later she made her way down to the bar feeling somehow better than she had in months.

"Hey Frankie!" Erin said joyfully.

"Hey Erin! What in the world? Looks like you had a good night last night. Who?"

"Tiffany. The blond who was asking all the questions."

"Well, I guess you got what you deserved for sleeping with a teenager," Frankie replied jokingly.

"You're just jealous!" Erin joked back. "Besides, she's twenty-two and it was a one time thing, never to be discussed again."

"Okay then, but you know you're old enough to be her mother." Frankie accused.

"Barely!" Erin shouted snapping Frankie in the ass with a bar towel.

"Whatever, I'm just happy to see you smile again," she replied before returning to her side of the bar.

# Chapter Eight

Abby was not totally surprised to wake up alone in the bed. She thought that perhaps Lauren needed some time to herself to work out whatever it was that she was going through. Abby was anxious to break things off with Lauren before they got too serious, but it appeared that Lauren was dealing with her own demons at the moment. It wouldn't be right to walk away now.

Lauren had been up since the crack of dawn driving around for hours with no specific purpose. Abby would no doubt be wondering where she was, but she wasn't quite ready to have that conversation yet. Yesterday had been too painful and she hadn't yet wrapped her head around the fact that Karen had manipulated the photos of Jules with that other woman to make it seem as though they were having an affair. Photos, that eventually resulted in their break-up after three blissful years together. Jules had been so adamant about her innocence, but Lauren had the proof, or so she thought.

She had even given Jules the opportunity to tell the truth and had agreed to work on their relationship, but when she wouldn't admit to it, Lauren threw her out. *Stupid Lauren. So stupid. She was the love of your life and had never given you any indication that she was cheating on you, but you believed Karen.* Just the thought of Karen made her want to vomit. *Well, at least she's out of my life for good now.*

It was nearly ten o'clock when Abby decided it was time enough for Lauren to come home and talk to her about what was going on. She picked up her cell phone and dialled Lauren's number.

"Hello sweetheart," Lauren said trying in vain to sound cheerful when she recognized the number on the call display.

"Are you okay?" Abby asked sincerely.

"I'm fine. Sorry if I worried you."

"Can you come home now? Please?"

"Already on my way, sweetheart," she replied before hanging up the phone and making a quick u-turn. Her head was pounding. She could not think anymore and hiding from Abby was not going to solve her problems.

"Hi," Lauren said sheepishly to the anxious-looking Abby, after arriving home a short while later.

"Hi to you," Abby replied allowing a smile to replace her frown as she slowly approached Lauren. She cupped Lauren's chin and lifted her head so their eyes met and then gently brushed the bruise under Lauren's eye before kissing her softly on the lips.

"Have you eaten yet?" Abby asked, trying to ease the tension that existed between them.

"No." Lauren replied.

"Well, let's see what I can scrounge up for you then."

"You can't do that; Cook will have your head!"

"No she won't," Abby said, smiling at the fact that Lauren had no idea that she'd won over the angry woman.

"Okay, but if she catches us, I'm blaming you."

Abby was happily preparing something for Lauren to eat when Cook walked in and caught them. Lauren turned white as a ghost waiting for the yelling to begin.

"Miss Abby, have you found everything you need, dear?" Cook said cheerfully.

Lauren sat open-mouthed at the interaction between the two women.

"Under control, Cook. I was just making something for our wayward friend here to eat."

"Good, Miss Lauren needs to eat. She forgets sometimes, you know," Cook replied as if Lauren wasn't even in the room with them.

"I'll be in my room if you need anything, dear!"

"Thanks Cook," Abby replied.

"See, I told you, nothing to worry about."

"How did you do that?" Lauren asked, amazed at Abby's ability to melt the miserable woman. "She's tossed more than one of my girlfriends out of her kitchen, not to mention me, on more than one occasion."

"She's actually a very nice woman, Lauren; you just have to treat her with respect. We've been keeping each other company in your absence."

A small grin appeared on her lips. "I see. So what has she told you about me that I should explain?" Lauren asked accusingly.

"Not much, though I tried. She just warned me about Karen mostly."

"Um. Karen won't be a problem anymore. I fired her yesterday and paid her a hefty settlement to get the hell out of my life."

"And did the black eye come before that or after that?" Abby asked sarcastically. She was unnaturally upset that someone had put their hands on Lauren.

"After, actually ... but it's over. I just have to move beyond some of the things she has done to me that have only recently come to light."

"Like what?" Abby said placing a plate of food in front of Lauren, kissing her softly on the top of her head.

"Like Jules," Lauren replied, then proceeded to tell Abby the whole sordid story of how Karen had confronted her with pictures of Jules and another woman in a precarious position and how she had ended their relationship because of it.

"This is really good, who taught you to cook?" Lauren said changing the subject for a minute trying to disguise the incredible hurt she was feeling about what happened with Jules.

"I just sort of picked it up on my own, I guess," Abby replied. "You really loved her, didn't you?"

"More than anything." Lauren admitted freely. "I feel like such a fool."

"It's not your fault Lauren. You did what you did because you thought it was the right thing to do with the knowledge you had at the time." Abby really didn't understand, but she wanted to sound supportive.

"I know, but it hurts all the same." Lauren closed her eyes for a moment, swallowed hard and decidedly changed the subject. "What else did Cook tell you?"

"Nothing really, but why don't you tell me a bit about your past. I realized yesterday that I know nothing about you except what I've read or seen on TV."

"What do you want to know exactly, you seem to be fishing for something specific?" she replied getting up from the table walking over to the sink to put her arms around Abby, who was busily washing dishes.

She was fishing, and she knew it. The picture of Lauren with Erin had unsettled her. She didn't know why, but she had to know their history.

"Oh, I don't know, tell me about Erin."

Lauren stepped away from Abby and smiled. "Somebody's been snooping around while I've been gone!" she teased.

Abby nodded as her face reddened in embarrassment.

"It's okay. I have nothing to hide, sweetheart." She thought the topic of Erin might come up for one reason or another.

"Then, tell me about it."

"She was my first ... and she was a wonderful lover ... the best," Lauren said thinking back to the wonderful times they had shared together. No one had ever pleased her so completely, so passionately. "She broke up with me after about a year because I had changed so much. Understandably so. We've remained friendly throughout the years, but nothing more."

"How many others have there been?" Abby wanted to ask more about Erin, but thought Lauren might become suspicious. Abby didn't even understand herself, why she wanted to know more.

"I'm not sure, to be quite honest. After Erin, I was with Jules for three years, Karen for about three, then, this last year ... has been a bit of a blur." She had been acting very irresponsibly lately. After being hurt badly at the end of her last two serious relationships, she had decided to avoid getting too intimate with anyone. Several one-night stands and a few short-term trysts later had sent her searching for love again. Love, she hoped she would find with Abby.

"Were you ever happy with Karen?" She couldn't fathom the two of them together. Lauren seemed so kind-hearted and caring. She was the complete opposite of the vengeful and sadistic Karen.

"I guess for a while, it seemed that way ... she was twisted though. I can't believe it took me so long to see her for what she really was." She shook her head in shame. "Good riddance!"

"How about you Abby, there was no mention of any long standing relationships in your file?"

"There haven't been any ... as a matter of fact, you, are the longest relationship I've had. I've never even been on a second date." She sounded proud of herself, but as she heard her own words, they made her sad.

"Wow, then you must feel like we're practically married by now, it's been nearly three whole days," Lauren replied sarcastically. "To what do I owe the honour of your continued presence?"

"Good sex, intellectual conversation and fantastic food." Abby joked not entirely sure herself why she was still there.

"Well, then," Lauren replied wrapping Abby in her arms, gazing seductively into her eyes. "Why don't I give you that special tour of the house I was talking about the other day?"

Abby was very happy that Lauren's mood had shifted. Lauren had been in such a terrible emotional state the last day and a half and Abby was having a difficult time dealing with it. She didn't know how to comfort her. The arrogance she had used to control and seduce Abby had disappeared and been replaced with a sullen darkness she feared Lauren would not break free from.

"Okay, but first I have a favour to ask?" Abby said pulling a few inches away from Lauren and placing her hands playfully on her chest.

"Ask away," Lauren said pulling her closer again causing Abby's heart to flutter.

She pushed away again. This was a serious discussion and she needed to focus. "This is important. I know tomorrow is our last day together, but I was wondering if you would mind if I borrowed your car and went out for the day?"

"Certainly, you can borrow my car." She pulled Abby close again enjoying this little game of cat and mouse and whispered in her ear, "But what could be more important than spending the day with me?"

"I want to go pay a visit to Helena Morris."

"Your mother!" Lauren said stepping away in surprise.

"Not my mother, the woman who gave birth to me. I do not have a mother."

"Come on, Abby, the file says your mother's estranged from the family, but surely you can't mean that."

"I haven't heard a word from her since the day she left. I didn't even know where she was until I saw it in my file."

"I didn't know, Abby. I'm sorry."

"No, it's okay. I think it's time I confront her."

"Why don't I go with you ... for moral support?"

"I think this is something I should do on my own." She didn't know how she would react to seeing her mother after all this time. Whatever display of emotion would result, she certainly did not want Lauren to witness it.

"Why don't we compromise? I'll drive you there, make sure everything is okay and then I'll leave until you want me to come pick you up. That way we can still spend most of the day together and I'll know you're okay."

"Are you sure you want to do that? I may not be the best company tomorrow."

"You couldn't possibly be worse company than I've been to you the last couple of days."

"It hasn't been that bad. It's just hard to imagine that the person you were last night is the same person you were two days ago. So different, it's scary."

"It's a little scary for me too ... Now, how about that tour?" she said changing the subject again.

"Lead on!" Abby exclaimed, knowing that Lauren wanted to drop the subject for good.

She reached her hand out for Lauren's as they left the kitchen, but they didn't make it past the first hallway before they were locked in an embrace that threatened to bring them both beyond the point of no return.

Lauren stopped them, pulling away slightly, "Not here, sweetheart, not like this. Follow me," she said urgently, taking Abby's hand and leading her to the first unoccupied room in the house, which was the library. She quickly shut and locked the door.

"But, I've already seen this room." Abby protested.

"Not from this angle," Lauren replied, forcing Abby back onto the sofa.

"How many rooms are there in this house?" Abby asked, slightly concerned that her stamina would be desperately lacking after only a few.

"Don't worry; we don't have to see the whole house today. We may never leave this room," Lauren replied, smiling as she helped Abby out of her clothes.

They spent the next three hours exploring each other and the rest of the room until they both collapsed on the sofa completely exhausted and temporarily satisfied. "I think I want more, but my body won't cooperate," Abby said through strained breaths.

"Good," Lauren said exhausted herself.

"Good that I want more or good that I'm exhausted?

"Both," Lauren replied cuddling into Abby's arms as they drifted off into sleep.

Abby woke first, enjoying for a few minutes, the sight of her lover sleeping peacefully. She gently brushed the bruise under Lauren's eye with her lips. Lauren woke with a start then relaxed and smiled up at Abby who looked down at her with such concern.

"Does it hurt?" Abby asked softly.

"Only when you touch it," she replied grimacing.

"Sorry."

"It's okay. Are you hungry, sweetheart?"

"Always," Abby replied.

They quickly got up and found their clothes, which had been scattered, about the room. Once dressed, they headed to the kitchen to find that Cook had prepared a special meal for them today, but since they were otherwise occupied, she had left it in the warmer. Lauren was amazed that Cook had gone through the trouble of keeping dinner warm. In the past, she would have just put it in the fridge or fed it to the staff. She had always insisted that Lauren be present when dinner was served because she didn't want to be held responsible for how it tasted after being kept warm for hours.

After enjoying their meal and a bottle of wine, they decided to take a walk along the path that led through the orchard. There was a slight chill in the air, but neither seemed to mind as they walked along in silence.

Abby's mind was occupied by thoughts of what tomorrow's reunion with her mother would bring. Could the woman say anything at all to justify what she had done? Abby could think of no logical reason for her behaviour. How could she just walk out on her child with no explanation?

Lauren could not help but let her mind wander to Jules. The awful look of disbelief on her face when she'd asked her to leave. Could she ever do anything to make up for hurting her so badly?

"Are you cold, Lauren?" Abby asked, noticing the goose bumps on her arms.

"A bit." The goose bumps had little to do with the temperature and a lot to do with the memories of Jules. "Maybe we should go back to the house. I'm a bit tired too and you have a big day tomorrow."

"Yeah, I guess so," Abby replied, taking Lauren's hand in hers as they walked back to the house.

# Chapter Nine

Lauren put the top down as they headed for I-5. It was about a two-hour drive to get to Bakersfield with traffic the way that it was. The warm sun mixed with the wind blowing through her hair was a welcome sensation. Her mind felt clear today and her only concern was Abby, who was sitting silently in the passenger seat. "Sweetheart, are you scared?" Lauren asked.

"I'm not sure what I feel … I'm kind of … numb. This whole trip may be a waste of time. She may not even be home," Abby replied sharply, gazing out the window.

"First of all, no amount of time we spend together, no matter what we are doing, is a waste of time, and secondly, don't you think announcing your intended visit may allow her time to prepare some sort of dignified response to her leaving."

"I was thinking the same thing. If I surprise her, I'm more likely to get the truth." Finally looking over to Lauren. "Thank you for going with me."

"My pleasure, sweetheart."

"It should be right up here," Lauren said slowing the car as they entered the subdivision to read the addresses on the homes. She stopped in front of the modest brick two storey home. "This is it. Ready?" She reached for Abby's hand and squeezed it gently.

"Ready, as I'll ever be," Abby said taking in a deep breath and stepping out of the car to make her way down the sidewalk to the door.

Lauren stood behind her as she rang the doorbell. A few moments later, a tall, silver-haired man answered the door with a start. He looked as if he had seen a ghost when he saw Abby. "Helena!" he yelled, still staring at Abby.

She appeared almost instantly at his side. "What is it, dear? Oh My! Abigail, is that you?" Helena Morris said, gripping her husband's arm for support, shocked at the sight of Abby standing on their porch. She wanted to invite Abby and her friend in, but was unable to make the words form in her mouth.

"Do you mind if we come in?" Abby said snapping them back into reality.

"Sorry, yes, please do come in."

Helena led the women into the living room and motioned for them to have a seat unable to get a grip on the reality that her daughter was there. She had hoped for this day for so long. She had prepared herself mentally. She had rehearsed every word she would say many times over; but now, the reality of it all was too much for her to handle. She quickly excused herself from the room and left her husband there alone with the two women as she retreated to the kitchen to try to gather her thoughts.

"Abby, my name is William Morris. I'm not sure if you remember me, it's been quite some time. You and your mother used to visit me at my cabin when you were a child." Bill said trying to open the lines of communication somehow, knowing full well this would be a very difficult and tense situation.

"First of all, Mr. Morris, I do not regard that woman as my mother and secondly, I have no recollection of you or your cabin," Abby replied sharply.

"I understand your resentment, Miss Grant," he said, taking their conversation back to a formal tone realizing that Abby was still extremely bitter. "However, you should know that there are two sides to every story and perhaps you should at least listen to what your mother has to say before you jump to any conclusions."

"Once again, Mr. Morris, she is not my mother and I have not jumped to any conclusions. I have had eleven years to come to my conclusions, plenty of time to form a complete appraisal of the facts."

Helena stood in the kitchen listening to the conversation between her husband and her daughter knowing that there was a possibility that no matter what she said, Abby might never forgive her. But she had to try and she couldn't hide from the truth any longer. She returned to the living room with a pitcher of water and some glasses, setting them down on the coffee table, before taking a seat across from her daughter.

Lauren, sensing the growing tension, filled a glass of water and handed it to Abby. She squeezed her hand trying to offer her strength and said softly, "I think I'll leave now, okay sweetheart?" Abby did not reply; she only stared blankly into the pitcher on the table as Mr. Morris escorted Lauren to the front door.

"Miss Waters!" he shouted as Lauren opened the door to step into her car. "Everything will be fine; I assure you and thank you for bringing her here."

"Abby came here of her own accord, Mr. Morris. I am only here to provide her support should she need it." He did not reply. He only nodded as Lauren got in the car and drove off.

"She's beautiful, Abby, I'm so happy you finally found someone," Helena said trying to strike up some sort of common ground to begin the conversation. She was surprised to see that her daughter was not alone when she arrived. Abby had grown into a beautiful woman so it was not a surprise that a woman of Lauren Waters' stature would find her attractive, it's just that no matter how many times she had rehearsed this reunion, Abby had always been alone. The fact that her daughter had not seemed to find someone to share her life with, often made her sad.

"Yes, she is," Abby agreed pointedly. "But what business is it of yours and what do you mean, finally found someone?" Abby was growing angrier by the minute. What gave this woman the right to have any happiness for her?

"Congratulations on your award the other day," Helena said trying to keep the conversation moving forward without drawing too much emotion.

"How do you know about it?"

"I was there, sitting in the back row; just like I was there at your high school graduation; just like I was there at your softball finals when you hit the homerun which brought in the winning runs for your team and just like I was there for every other important moment in your life," she said matter-of-factly.

Abby was in shock. Had her own mother been stalking her? Why had she never announced herself? All these years. "Am I supposed to be impressed that you followed me around for ten years?" Abby replied harshly.

"No, Abigail. I just wanted to let you know that I was always there for you."

"There for me! You were never there for me. You left me. You abandoned me. You didn't even care enough to tell me you were leaving …"

Helena interrupted, "That's where you're wrong Abigail. I loved you so much, it was the best thing I could do for you at the time."

"I don't understand. How can walking out on your child be the best thing for them?"

"Do you remember the night I left, Abby?"

Abby searched her mind for the memory. She had come home and remembered a great deal of tension between her parents, but it was the same day as her affair with Mrs. Jones and she was too preoccupied to concern herself with anything else at that point. She had gone to her room, turned on her stereo and, when she got up the next morning, her mother was gone. She nodded at her mother.

"Did you see anything when you came through the door?" Helena questioned. Abby thought back and shook her head no. "I had a gun pointed at your father Abby. I was going to shoot him," Helena said painfully. Abby sat perfectly still listening to the unbelievable. "I was tired of his constant affairs, it was bad enough that he continued them, but when he started flaunting them in my face, telling me to leave so he could bring some woman home, I couldn't take it anymore. I had wanted to leave him many years earlier, but he wouldn't let me take you. He said if I wanted to go, I could, but that if I took you with me, it would be over his dead body. I stayed until I thought you were old enough to take care of yourself because lord knows he wouldn't have been able to take care of you. Over the years I only grew to resent him more."

"He never loved me. The only reason we married in the first place was because my father insisted on it when I got pregnant. When I finally decided to leave, I was determined to take you with me, you were already starting to look up to him and I did not want you to end up cold and heartless like he was." Helena stopped for a moment to catch her breath. She was happy her daughter hadn't interrupted her to this point. She had to get it all out.

"When you walked in while I had the gun pointed at him it snapped me back into reality. As much as I hated the man, I couldn't shoot him. He was still your father and you would never have forgiven me for that. I would have gone to jail and you would have lost both your parents. When I put the gun away, he told me that if I ever tried to contact you he would tell you what I did and then have me arrested. I left immediately and checked myself into a psychiatric ward for a couple of weeks, shortly after that, I moved in with Bill and we've been together ever since."

Both women sat in complete silence for what seemed like forever. Helena finally broke the silence. "Abby, do you have any questions about what I just told you?"

Abby stated blankly at her mother as she asked, "Were you and Bill having an affair the whole time I was a child?"

"No, we were just friends for the first few years. It wasn't until you were about fourteen when it progressed to something more. He's a very good man, a very loving, caring man who treats me like a woman should be treated. You used to like going to his cabin when you were a child. When we got there I used to have the hardest time getting you to come home with me."

"I don't remember. Why can't I remember?"

"Abby, do you remember much of your life before the night I left?"

Abby searched her memories and was unable to find any. "No, not really," she replied.

"I think maybe you saw more that night than you want to remember," Helena said suggesting that Abby had indeed seen her pointing a gun at her father and that she had repressed that memory along with all the memories that led up to that night.

"Helena, I think I should leave now," Abby said dialling Lauren's number as she spoke.

"I understand Abby, this must be overwhelming. Just know that I've always loved you and I only did what I thought was best for you." She wanted so much to put her arms around her daughter, but Abby was not ready to forgive her yet. It would take time, it could possibly take forever, but at least she had told her side of the story.

Abby walked out of the house and waited in the driveway for Lauren. She was in shock. Her head was spinning, her stomach churning. To think that her mother hated her father so much she wanted to kill him. No wonder he didn't want to get involved in a relationship.

"Hi sweetheart, how did it go?" Lauren asked sincerely.

Abby did not reply; she stared blankly ahead as Lauren started up the interstate. Lauren didn't ask again. She knew that Abby was probably trying to sort things out in her head. She also knew that although they had become closer over the last few days, they really didn't know each other that well and she did not expect Abby to confide in her.

As Lauren drove, she tried to figure out what the next logical step would be to her and Abby's relationship. Clearly, this was not the time to discuss it, but she knew they would have to at some point. She sensed that Abby did not want to commit to anything, which upset her at first, but now, there was something else tugging at her heartstrings. It was Jules. She wouldn't expect her forgiveness, but if there was the slightest chance that they could be together again, maybe it would be best if things didn't get too serious with Abby. It wasn't so much that Abby was second best, it was just that the circumstances had changed. A few days ago, it had been her intention to make Abby fall in love with her. She was tired of the endless plethora of women who had come in and out of her life during the last year. She was looking to settle down with someone and she knew, from the very first moment, that Abby would be the one.

About fifteen minutes from home Abby finally spoke. "I'm sorry, Lauren," she said.

"No need to be sorry, sweetheart. Are you okay? Do you want to talk about it?" Lauren asked. She was caught so off guard when Abby finnaly spoke that she didn't know what to say to her or how to comfort her.

"I'm okay, I think," Abby said taking Lauren's hand into hers seeking the comfort and strength that only Lauren could provide her at that moment. Lauren pulled the car over and took Abby's hands in hers, looking into her eyes for an instant before pulling her close for a hug. Abby needed this, but did not want to cry in front of Lauren, so she pulled away after only a few minutes, ashamed of her weakness.

"Let's go home," Abby suggested, fighting back the tears that were threatening.

When they walked through the door Abby immediately asked Lauren to take her upstairs to bed. She needed the intimacy, but wanted the sex as a distraction. Lauren obliged, remembering how Abby had done the same for her a few nights earlier.

"Lauren?" Abby said after she regained her composure.

"Yes, sweetheart?"

"Thank you."

They were nearly silent on the way to the airport. Both women wondering what the other was thinking and knowing deep down that they would probably never see each other again.

"Thanks Lauren. I had a great time."

"Me too!" There was nothing more for either woman to say. Lauren was determined to find Jules and beg for her forgiveness. Abby was going back to her uncomplicated, solitary life.

The air was crisp and cold as Abby made her way from the terminal to her car. It was snowing heavily and she was thankful that she had decided to fly out of Lansing instead of driving to Detroit. With this snow, it would have taken her hours to get home and at this very moment, she wanted nothing more than to get home and get back to her life, as she knew it.

Despite the snow, the roads were clear and Abby was walking through her front door twenty-five minutes later. She did not bother to unpack or check her messages. She headed directly for the shower, hoping to wash away any remnants of her trip to LA. She crawled into bed, praying for the familiarity to consume her. She tossed and turned for hours. Thoughts of Erin, haunting her, every time she closed her eyes. She took a sleeping pill and finally fell asleep.

She groaned when her alarm sounded only a few hours later at 6:00 AM. She didn't want to go to work. She was exhausted, mentally and physically. She did not want to speak to her father. She did not want to speak to anyone, but she also knew that getting back to work was the quickest way to get on with her life.

Pulling into her parking spot, she was completely unaware of how she got to work, but she felt a little bit relieved to be back. She was grateful to see that her father had not yet arrived and was hoping that perhaps she would not have to see him today. She turned on her computer, and stared angrily at the enormous pile of work on her desk. Was there no one else capable of taking on some of these responsibilities? Her email inbox was nearly full and she had twenty-five voice mail messages.

    She dove into her work, determined to push the recurring thoughts of Erin from her head.

# Chapter Ten

Abby was unable to avoid her father the following day. He walked right into her office first thing in the morning with a bouquet of red roses.

"Who are those from?" she questioned.

"I don't know, they're for you and I didn't think I should read the card."

Abby took the flowers from him and set them on the corner of her desk. She opened the card and stared questioningly at the words.

*I'm truly sorry. You'll see it soon enough. Lauren*

"Well, are you going to tell me who they're from?" Carson Grant asked.

"Just someone I met in L.A., Dad. No need to worry about it," Abby said innocently. She had no idea what the note meant and now was not the time to try to decipher it.

"Okay then, I won't. Are you keeping up with all the work coming in Abby?" he asked, concerned at the enormous amount of work sitting on his daughter's desk.

"I'm trying to. It's just that I've got a week's worth of catching up to do and we seem to get busier everyday." Abby was trying not to complain, but she knew she clearly took on a much bigger workload than anyone else and it was starting to bother her.

"If you want to hire an assistant, you are more than welcome to. You look like you could use some help and I was thinking about hiring a junior person around here anyways because things are starting to get a little overwhelming for everyone."

"I'll keep that in mind," Abby said, knowing that her father would not think less of her for doing so, but at the same time, she wanted to prove that she could do it alone.

"Hey Dad!" she said as he reached the door, "I saw Helena while I was gone."

"I know," he replied not the least bit surprised.

"You talked to her?" Abby asked in amazement.

"I speak with your mother quite frequently, Abby. How do you think she knows all those things about you?"

"You told her where I'd be?"

"Abby, listen, over the last few years, your mother and I have kept in touch. There was 1 time, when you were about twenty-one, that I had no idea what to do with you. You were wild. You were out drinking and partying and I was lost. So I called your mother for advice."

"I can't believe I'm only finding out about all of this now!" Abby shouted as she left her office and went outside to get some air. Carson followed her out, but did not say anything. He just stood beside his daughter and waited for her to speak. He was relieved when she finally did.

"Dad, why didn't you tell me sooner?" Abby asked tears streaming down her face.

"We thought it was for the best, Abby. By the time we were on speaking terms, your mother and I decided that you probably wouldn't understand and that if and when you were ready, you would track her down." He looked down to his feet before continuing. "I guess we could have handled the whole situation better. I should have let your mother take you. You would have been much better off."

"Dad, don't blame yourself, she's the one who pointed the gun at you."

"I deserved it. I did so many terrible things to your mother; it's a miracle that she even speaks to me at all," he said convincingly as he looked directly into Abby's eyes.

"I think I'm going to work from home the rest of the day. I need to think."

Carson gave his daughter a hug, something he rarely did, and sent her on her way.

Abby was overwhelmed with a sense of confusion. The life she had been living had suddenly become unexpectedly different. That which she thought was so; was not. That which she thought she wanted; she did not. So many thoughts were racing through her mind at the same time; she was unable to focus on any one of them.

She knew she was pushing herself too hard as she completed her fifth set of leg extensions; her muscles screaming at her, sweat streaming down her face. She would pay for this tomorrow, she knew, but today, the pain she was feeling was helping to clear her mind.

After a long shower, she was still not able to concentrate and the clear night was allowing the moonlight to reflect off the snow, inviting her to go for a long walk. Her wet hair was frozen solid by the time she returned to the house, but she didn't care.

The drive down to San Bernardino had been long. Erin suddenly wished she had gone to Dinah's to retrieve her bike. When she left, she took only her car and a bag of clothes. She had not gone back for anything else and this very minute the thought of the wind blowing against her body as she rode down the highway was calling to her. She had not been able to escape the memory of Abby. No woman had every touched her so deeply so quickly and although she thought it would get easier over time, each day her yearning grew stronger.

She pulled off to the side of the highway seeking the next closest thing and carefully removed the t-tops from her nineteen-eighty Transam. The wind now blowing through her hair, the stereo turned up as loud as it would go she tried to escape her own life, drowning in the wind and music.

"Mom, I'm feeling better, really, you don't have to keep fussing over me," Erin said sitting across from her mother as they prepared dinner for the rest of the family.

"Erin, dear, you need to start living again. You're so withdrawn. Why don't you start dating again? Maybe you'll meet someone. Someone who will make you happy."

"Mom please! I'm not ready to start dating again. I'm doing better. I don't need someone in my life right now." Jeez, she thought to herself, look what happened to her when she did try to meet someone new. Her life was turned upside down in a single evening. She wondered to herself why Tiffany had no lasting impression on her. She shook the memory of Abby from her mind as her mother continued her obligatory rant.

"Okay, but you know Mrs. Jacobs' daughter is single right now. Maybe you could just meet her for coffee or something?"

"No Mom! No blind dates. When I'm ready, I'll start dating again. Until then, please don't interfere."

"It would hardly be a blind date, Erin. You know the Jacobs girl. She's a very nice girl," her mother pledged.

"She's not my type," Erin replied angrily.

"Okay, don't get upset, dear. I just worry about you. Have you at least thought about letting little Meg move in with you?"

"Yes Mom, I've thought about it"

"And what have you decided?"

"It might be a good idea; I'll talk to her when she gets here tonight and see how we get along. It's not always easy living with someone, but it might be fun."

"Good, at least you won't be alone then."

"Meg and I are going to take a walk," Erin said as soon as she finished drying the last of the dishes.

"Okay dear, but don't be too long. You know I don't like you girls being out late at night. I worry you know," Mrs. Davis said in her usual motherly way.

"We'll be fine, Mom. I'm not a child anymore; you need to quit worrying about me," Erin said despite the fact that she knew her mother would worry no matter what she was doing.

As the two women walked and talked, they learned a great deal about each other. Meg confided in Erin about the reasons behind her decision to attend Cal State instead of staying in North Dakota. Her parents had been fighting a lot and she wanted to get away from that as far as possible. Her older brother had already moved out and now it was only her and her parents and she felt stuck in the middle. Erin felt bad for her niece, but was not at all surprised that her brother John was having marital problems. She had often thought that he and his bride made an unsuitable couple. He was well grounded and she was very much a free spirit. When they married, each expected the other to change and over the last twenty years, neither of them had.

Meg also seemed very interested in animation and Cal State had an excellent program for that. She must have got the creativity from her mother's side of the family since neither Erin nor John had a creative bone in their bodies.

Erin was honest with Meg about Dinah when she asked. She had been about fourteen when she had finally asked Erin about her sexuality and ever since she had accepted any of Erin's girlfriends into the family and insisted on calling them aunt so and so. Meg was the only person Erin called when she and Dinah broke up. Meg had kept her secret all along and for that, she was eternally grateful.

"So if you want to live with me; you have to follow a few simple rules." Erin spoke sternly to her eighteen-year-old niece.

"Number one ... no men spend the night. I'm not a prude. Just go spend the night at their house. I don't want to wake up to my toilet seat up one morning. I just don't want to deal with it."

"Okay," Meg replied with a giggle. "What's rule number two?"

"You must be respectful to anyone I bring home."

"Oh! So it's okay for you to bring some woman home, but not okay for me."

"You can bring a woman home for the night, just not a man." Erin chuckled knowing that's not what Meg meant by her statement.

"That's not what I mean and you know it."

"It's my place. Ergo my rules. Take it or leave it. And two more things. No parties, unless I agree, and I'm not cleaning up after you."

"Okay, Aunt Erin. When can I move in?" Meg asked excitedly.

"As soon as you want," Erin replied suddenly feeling elated at the fact that she would have a roommate to keep her company.

Abby dragged her aching body through her office door and collapsed into her chair. Since she hardly ever got sick, she was a wuss when she caught a cold. She went home early the other day and didn't even bother getting out of bed yesterday. The stress of the last couple of weeks must have caught up with her, weakening her naturally resilient immune system.

She was upset to find her desk piled high with work again. She had only missed a day and a half of work, but it seemed as if everyone who was behind on a project dumped it off on her while she was gone and unable to refuse it. This had to stop. Abby knew she had created her own nightmare with the people she worked with. She had never said no when anyone handed off projects to her because she wanted to be able to do it all. Somehow, she wanted to prove herself to her father, but now, she was dangerously close to missing deadlines and that would definitely not impress him.

Abby began reading through the stack of resumes that had come in the month before. Rarely did they ever use resumes that came in unsolicited, but she needed help now, not a month from now, which would be how long it would take to hire someone the traditional way. She was nearly through the stack when a familiar name caught her eye, Hailey Jean Janson. Hailey, of course! Why hadn't she thought of her earlier? They got along well. She was well qualified and Hailey had indicated that she wasn't happy working where she was, and that she was only staying there until something better came along. Perfect! Abby was too impatient to leave a message on Hailey's home phone so she searched her cell phone for the number. Hailey was adamant about putting her number in Abby's phone and Abby had forgotten to delete it. Locating the number, Abby quickly pushed dial and unceremoniously dumped the remainder of the resumes in the trashcan.

"Hailey Janson!"

"Hailey, hi, um it's Abby … Abby Grant. I'm not sure if you remember me or not?" Abby said anxiously.

"How could I ever forget Abby, 'one time only' Grant?" Hailey teased.

"Okay, I guess I deserved that."

"What can I do for you, Abby? Are you really dating Lauren Waters?"

"How do you know about Lauren?" Abby questioned.

"Don't you read the tabloids? There's a picture of you and Lauren outside of some mall."

"Shit! Well at least that explains the note she sent me."

"What's she like? I've always had a crush on her. I can't believe you're with her."

"I'm not with her. I spent a few days with her. That's all, and I didn't call to talk about her," Abby said trying to focus on the reason for her call. "I called to ask you if you were free for dinner; there's something I'd like to discuss with you."

"I guess I have time for dinner. You're not going to tell me what this is about are you?"

"Nope." Abby laughed, "I'll pick you up at six."

"I'll be waiting," Hailey said hanging up the phone.

Abby knew she had better track her father down and let him know about her plans with Hailey. She also knew that she would have to come clean about Lauren as well. A discussion she was not looking forward to. Her thoughts were interrupted by a quick knock on the door and a boisterous co-worker who shouted, "Way to go Abby! You're the man!" He grinned and gave her the thumbs up. *Men are such pigs,* she mumbled to herself. The word was spreading quickly now so she had to face the daunting task of meeting with her father. She gathered her composure and quickly walked down the long narrow hall to her father's office. She waited at the door as he finished his phone call before entering his office and closing the door.

"Abigail! You've been avoiding me since our talk a few weeks ago. What brings you by?"

"Sorry, Dad. I just needed some time to think. I gather you've heard the latest gossip?"

"I understand Abby; I just thought you would have filled me in. You know I don't like to hear about things second-hand."

"I know. I wasn't expecting to have my face plastered across a tabloid. I haven't even seen it yet." Abby paused, looking at the disappointment on her father's face before continuing. "There's really nothing going on between us."

"What's she like? Is she as nice in person as she appears to be?"

"She's great; she's so down to earth that you forget who she is when you're with her." Abby stopped. She was getting sidetracked. "Honestly though, I doubt I'll ever see her again."

She tried to refocus on why she was there. "I was thinking that maybe I should hire someone to give me a hand. It's starting to be too much."

"It's about time, Abby. You know you can't do it all yourself. And don't think I haven't noticed everyone dumping work on you while you're gone. If you hadn't decided to hire someone soon, I was going to do it for you. Do you have anyone in mind?"

"There's a woman I met a while ago. Her name is Hailey Janson. She graduated last year and has been working at K & M doing grunt work since then. I know she's ready to get the hell out of there. She's tired of the bullshit. She seems to have some good ideas and just wants the opportunity to prove herself."

"If you think you can work with her; pay her what you think she's worth and get her in here as soon as possible. Don't wait until you bury yourself so deep that you can't get out."

"Thanks Dad"

"Get back to work!" He chuckled as he motioned for Abby to leave his office.

# Chapter Eleven

Abby spent the rest of the afternoon trying to prioritize the projects on her desk. She would have to do some work from home if she was going to get them all completed so she separated the projects into two piles; the ones that she could work on at home and the ones she couldn't.

She was really looking forward to dinner with Hailey. So much so, that she had all but forgotten her cold.

She was unusually excited as she pulled into the parking lot of Hailey's apartment building. Hailey's green eyes sparkled when she opened the door and greeted Abby with a warm smile. She was dressed in a flattering pair of faded blue jeans that hung low, accentuating her thin frame and a blue and red rugby shirt. Her sandy blond hair was longer than Abby remembered, but it was still ruffled and unruly showing off her playful side.

"Hello Hailey!" Abby said, suddenly feeling a little bit shy.

"Hi Abby. I really didn't think I'd ever see you again. You made it quite clear that you weren't interested," Hailey said sarcastically.

"That's not why I'm here, Hailey. Not that I didn't enjoy our evening together. I asked you to dinner because I have a proposition for you. We can talk about it when we get there. Are you ready?"

"Little defensive aren't we?" Hailey responded harshly.

"Maybe a little. Are you ready to go? I'm starving. I thought we could go to Papa Joe's; I'm dying for some good pizza."

"Sounds good to me," Hailey exclaimed, very pleased with Abby's choice of restaurant. She had been craving a good pizza for a couple of weeks and Papa Joe's was the best in town.

"I'm ready; just let me lock the patio door."

Abby admired Hailey as they made their way down to the parking lot. She was very attractive and had a great personality. Abby could definitely see herself working with Hailey on a daily basis; she could also see herself becoming good friends with Hailey; something she had never wanted to do with anyone before. She was certain they would argue a lot, but that they would be able to keep work at work and maintain a solid friendship outside of work; their personalities seemed well suited to that type of relationship.

Papa Joe's was a small Italian restaurant that catered to the college crowd. It usually didn't get busy until after eight o'clock so they arrived at the perfect time to get a table by the window, not that there was anything to look at outside in the middle of winter. In the spring, the street outside the restaurant would be busy with the bustle of students walking up and down Main Street. This night, however, the view would serve as a gentle distraction should the conversation become uncomfortable.

Abby found Hailey's tomboyish qualities intriguing. She was amazed when Hailey ordered them a pitcher of beer and a large pepperoni pizza without even asking her opinion. Hailey was definitely not Abby's usual type and she pondered for a moment why she had even picked Hailey up at the bar the night they met. They certainly had a lot in common though. Perhaps that night several weeks ago was a result of her inner-self, reaching out to find what she had been missing all of these years.

"So, are you going to tell me why I'm here?" Hailey finally asked.

"Yeah, I guess it's the least I could do since you agreed to have dinner with me. I was a bit concerned you would have turned me down."

"I probably should have, but my curiosity got the better of me, I guess."

"Are you still at K & M?"

"Unfortunately," Hailey replied. "I've applied at a few other places, but no one wants to hire a woman. They say it tends to complicate the working relationship. I think it's just the male ego that can't take the fact that some women are more than capable of designing things as well as them."

"Yeah, I think you're right. They hate it when a woman becomes more successful than they do. Besides that, they're always trying to find a way to get in your pants," she added laughingly.

"You mean to tell me that if you had some hot, sexy, young woman working with you everyday you wouldn't try to get in her pants?"

"Should we try to find out?" Abby asked, knowing Hailey probably wouldn't catch the subtleness of the job offer.

"What?"

"How would you like to come and work with me over at CG?" Abby asked seriously.

"Are you serious? You're offering me a job?" Hailey asked. "Don't play games with me Abby. Is this for real?" she added cautiously, still not believing what she was hearing.

"Yes, Hailey, it's very much for real. We have an opening and I thought you'd be perfect for the position. And since I've already gotten into your pants once, I know I wouldn't have to try very hard to do it again," Abby said jokingly, trying to get Hailey to relax.

"Oh really! You think it would be that easy do you?" Hailey challenged teasingly.

"If my memory serves me correctly, I believe the word amazing was used to describe my abilities," Abby replied arrogantly.

"Yes, you were that; but what about Lauren?" she questioned.

"What about her? I told you I'm not seeing her. Besides, sex isn't part of the job description, I was only suggesting that perhaps, if the mood struck and we were both unattached, that we could maybe have some fun once in a while," Abby suggested gazing into Hailey's green eyes.

"Um! Friends with benefits and a new job. I'm so glad I agreed to let you take me to dinner tonight," Hailey replied smiling, gazing back into Abby's eyes.

"So, you'll take the job then?" Abby asked.

"On one condition. Work stays at work and whatever else happens stays outside of work."

"Deal! Don't you even want to know what you'll be paid?" Abby asked sincerely.

"Don't really care," she replied picking up the bill from the table.

"I asked you to dinner Hailey, it's my treat," she said trying to grab the bill from Hailey's hand.

"You can treat me in an hour or so when we get back to my place," Hailey said seductively. Abby bit back a response delighted in how the evening had progressed. Hailey had not only agreed to take the job, she was also willing, and eager to help satisfy Abby's personal needs. Perfect. She hadn't expected Hailey to take her up on that part of the offer, but if she was willing, then why not? Besides Abby knew Hailey was a great catch and she probably would not have this luxury for very long. Someone who would love her and treat her well would eventually come along. Abby was also certain that Hailey would not develop feelings beyond friendship for her so the potential complication of love would not become a factor. Hailey was well grounded and seemed very capable of separating sex and love.

"So when can you start?" Abby asked on the way back to Hailey's.

"When do you want me to start?"

"As soon as you can."

"If it was up to me, I'd start tomorrow, but I wouldn't feel right not giving them at least until Friday," Hailey replied sincerely.

"So, you're thinking Monday, then?"

"Yes, if that's okay. They may just escort me out on the spot tomorrow when I tell them I'm leaving, and in that case, I'll just start right away."

"So, are you going to come up or what?" Hailey asked when she pulled into the parking lot.

"Are you sure about this? You know I can't offer you more than occasional sex and friendship," Abby replied trying to make sure Hailey understood exactly where things stood before leaving the car.

"I'm very familiar with what you can and cannot offer and I'm perfectly content with occasional sex and friendship; as long as the sex is as good as it was the first time." Hailey chuckled excitedly.

"It won't be," Abby replied seriously "It will be better, much better," she added, stepping out of the car to follow Hailey into the building.

Abby was not at all surprised to find Hailey's apartment to be impeccably clean as it was the night of their first encounter. It was small, but tastefully decorated and it was close to work. Only about a ten-minute drive. An added bonus if a little afternoon delight should be in the cards some day.

Abby made herself at home on the couch as Hailey grabbed a couple of beers from the fridge and playfully plopped herself down in Abby's lap. Abby took a long swig of beer and looked deeply into Hailey's green eyes. Seeing nothing but want and desire she reached her hand behind Hailey's neck and pulled her in for a long, hot, sensual kiss. After a few moments, the two women pulled apart finishing their beer as they tried to catch their breath. Abby took the initiative once the beer was gone to firmly push Hailey down on the couch and kissed her hard on the lips giving way to the sudden wave of passion she was feeling. Hailey moaned in response to the pleasure, but put her hand up to stop Abby.

"Wait … take me to bed … there's more room on the bed." Hailey managed to say despite her growing need.

Abby quickly obliged, her strong body easily carrying Hailey to the bed. Abby wasted no time undressing Hailey, her need for pleasure driving her to move more quickly than she would have normally. Abby quickly disrobed under the watchful eye of her waiting partner before joining her under the covers. Hailey was insatiable, her orgasm lasting several minutes under the careful direction of Abby's skilled tongue. Abby rested her head against the soft skin of Hailey's stomach until her breathing returned to a more normal rhythm. Moments later, Abby was shocked at her own orgasm. Hailey had barely touched her. She came hard and fast surprising both herself and Hailey who seemed slightly disappointed. "Sorry," Abby said breathlessly. "It sort of snuck up on me," she added as she closed her eyes and let her mind wander as her body relaxed.

Hailey was lying next to her, looking at her when she finally opened her eyes a few minutes later. "What?" she asked at Hailey's questioning expression.

"Who are you thinking about? Is it Lauren?" she asked curiously. Abby shook her head no. She had been thinking about Erin again.

"There's someone else, isn't there? What happened to you in L.A.? What happened to your one night only rule?"

"Nothing happened to me and there isn't anyone else." Abby lied hoping Hailey would simply give up this pattern of questioning.

"There's something you're not telling me, Abigail Grant, and although I may not get it out of you today; I will find a way to make you tell me."

"I should get going," Abby replied.

"You don't have to leave you know, you're welcome to spend the night if you want." Hailey offered knowing Abby would still decline.

"Thanks anyway, but I'm going home." Abby said before kissing Hailey softly on the cheek and getting out of bed. "You'll call me tomorrow and let me know what your boss says, right?"

"Yeah. Can I have your cell phone number now so I can reach you directly?" she asked grabbing her own cell phone off the nightstand. Instead of her full name, Hailey typed ABS into her phone and handed it to Abby to type in the number.

"ABS?" she said looking at Hailey questioningly.

"What? Have you seen your stomach? You have the most amazing body; it's the perfect nickname for you." Abby did not answer; she only shook her head and finished punching in her phone number before giving the phone back to Hailey. One more kiss on the cheek and she was gone.

Hailey's boss had done as she expected; escorting her out the minute she told him she was taking the job at CG Designs. She began her new job that very afternoon and the next few weeks went by quickly. Hailey was fitting in very well with the group; laughing and joking with everyone. She seemed happy working there; arriving on time every day, smiling, staying late when needed without question. She had even suggested that they pay her less until she proved herself, but Abby wouldn't hear of it. She helped Abby catch up on all the outstanding projects and had begun taking on her own. Because of the amount of time they were spending together, they were quickly becoming good friends, something Abby thought she didn't want. Their rendezvous' had become somewhat of a regular occurrence and Hailey seemed as happy with the arrangement as Abby.

"Well Meg, this is it. Your new home! What do you think?" Erin said opening the door to the loft.

"It's umm … well; I guess I would say empty, Aunt Erin. And maybe dark, dismal, dreary, sad …"

"Okay, okay, enough!" Erin interrupted. "I know it's a little impersonal, but I have everything I need, and I just haven't felt much like sprucing the place up. There's been no reason to."

"Impersonal? It's more than that; it's barren. Tell me that you're not still hung up on Dinah?" Meg asked critically as she set her duffle bag down on the floor and looked Erin square in the eyes.

"Dinah! God no. I got over her months ago," Erin replied credibly.

"If not Dinah, then what? Why haven't you moved on? Frankie says you're not dating and it's not like you haven't had a ton of offers. You could have your pick of any woman who walks through the door, so what's really going on?"

"First of all, it's none of Frankie's business and secondly, maybe I don't want just any woman. Maybe I'm waiting for the right woman. Someone special, who can make me laugh. Someone who challenges me, and pushes me, to be better than I am. Someone who makes me feel safe and whole." She stopped knowing she had already revealed more than she had planned.

"We all want to meet someone like that, Aunt Erin, but how will you know if you never take the time to get to know any of them." She paused for a moment before continuing. "Unless, maybe, you've already met her?" She accused. "That's it, isn't it? Who is she?" Meg continued not letting her aunt off the hook.

Erin had mixed feelings about talking to Meg about this. She hadn't talked to anyone about Abby, not even Frankie, but somehow she felt compelled to talk to Meg. She had to discuss it with someone. It was driving her crazy. As much as she had tried, she couldn't stop thinking about Abby.

"You know me too well, Megan," Erin replied not sure how to bring it up. "There is someone, but it's complicated, and I don't think she feels the same way. Besides, she's seeing someone else."

"Complicated how?" Meg asked curiously.

"Here," Erin replied giving Meg the tabloid picture of Lauren and Abby that she kept folded in her pocket. "This is her."

"Lauren Waters? You want her back? Didn't you break up with her like ten years ago?"

"Yes. I mean no. Yes, I broke up with her, but no, I don't want her back. It's Abby, the other woman."

"Wow, she's hot. How do you know her?"

"It's a long story Meg, and unfortunately I have to get to work so it will have to wait," she said as she went into the bathroom to finish getting ready for work. "Oh, and Meg, no one knows about this. Not Frankie, not your mother and certainly not your grandmother. Do you understand me?" she added earnestly, making sure her niece understood that their conversation was confidential.

"Yes, Aunt Erin. It will stay between us. I kept quiet about you and Dinah remember?" Meg replied trying to convince her aunt that she could keep a secret. It had been difficult to keep her break-up with Dinah quiet for all those months, but she respected her aunt immensely so she did it.

"I remember and I trust you; I just wanted to make it clear that you are the only one who knows," she said giving her niece a big hug before walking out the door to start her shift.

Meg looked around the empty space, looked back down at the picture of Abby, and tried to make sense of the situation. There was no question she was an attractive woman, but her aunt had never put much emphasis on that sort of thing. There had to be more to this story. She was so affected by this woman, who seemed to be nothing more than a stranger. A stranger, who was dating Lauren Waters.

She carried her duffle bag to her room and began unpacking. Her room, although furnished, was as empty as the rest of the place. Her parents had purchased her this new bedroom set online and it had been delivered and set up last week before her arrival. Aside from the queen size bed, a nightstand and a large double dresser, there was nothing else in the room. She wished she had brought more than just a bag of clothes with her, but her parents had suggested that she just pack up everything and they would drive down to see her in a week or so once she was settled and bring her belongings. At least it would feel more like home if she had some of her things with her. The place was so sterile it was hard to believe it was anyone's home, especially her aunt's. Her aunt had always been so vibrant and full of life that it was hard to see her this way. She seemed so defeated and withdrawn it was like looking at someone she didn't even know.

Over the next few days, Meg had made it her sole purpose to bring some life into this dismal loft whether her aunt wanted her to or not. She would go out shopping during the day for supplies and while Erin was at work, she would busy herself painting the walls in beautiful, rich vibrant tones. Although her aunt never said a word, she could tell that she was pleased with it. She had purchased some canvas at the art supply store down the street and had made several paintings to hang on the walls. Most of which where of womanly forms in soothing embraces. They were soft and charming and when hung on the walls, brought the living room to life.

She added a few houseplants and at last was finished. She had revived her bedroom, the living room and the kitchen from their dismal past and brought them out of the wretched darkness to breathe and live amongst the inhabitants. The only room she had not dared touch was her aunt's bedroom, but to her surprise, a few days later, it was her aunt, herself, who had asked her to please do something with it. Meg was delighted, and joyfully did as requested, turning it into a lively, exciting space as well. It was as if the transformation of her living space had also affected her aunt because she seemed happier, her mood lighter, her smile real rather than forced. Meg had indeed accomplished what she had set out to do. Now, the only thing left to do was find a woman that would make her aunt happy.

# Chapter Twelve

"I'm glad you're feeling better. We've got a lot of work to catch up on," Abby said greeting Hailey as she walked through the door to her office. Hailey had been out for three days with the flu and the work had been piling up. It was clear that she still wasn't one hundred percent, but she did look a whole lot better than she did a couple of days ago.

"I'm just glad to be back. I was going crazy sitting at home by myself. Thanks for stopping by the other day and for cleaning up and everything. It was a big help. Give me ten minutes to check my messages and I'll be back and we can get up to speed," Hailey said before heading to her office down the hall.

She returned a half-hour later with a puzzled look on her face. "Abs? Do you know where the Carlysle data is?"

"It's in my briefcase." She pointed. "Over there."

Hailey fumbled with the briefcase spilling its contents on the floor causing Abby to chuckle as she went about her work otherwise unaffected by Hailey's clumsiness. Hailey carefully gathered the contents from the floor and began to sort through them until she found the file she was looking for. Happy to have found it amongst the mess, she cautiously set it aside and continued to replace the contents of the briefcase stopping suddenly when she came across a battered cocktail napkin. Discreetly she read the words and thought twice before asking about it.

"Abs? Who is Erin?" she asked innocently, holding the napkin up to Abby for her to see.

"Where did you get that?" Abby gasped. Although she had thought many times about that night, she had looked for that napkin and had not been able to find it. She had wanted to read it, to touch it. It was the only thing she had that tied her to Erin, and she thought it forever lost.

"It was in your briefcase. I guess it fell out when I dropped it," Hailey said shyly in response to Abby's sudden discomfort.

Abby did not speak. She rose from her chair, took the napkin from Hailey's hand, and delicately placed it on the desk. There before her, the simple, but carefully written note sat; the one thing that had changed her life forever and that she could not seem to forget. She gently brushed her finger over the words and closed her eyes remembering the moment Erin smiled at her; remembering the moment they kissed, remembering the feeling of waking up with her in her arms. She blushed at the memories and tried to will them away. Only when Hailey spoke did she open her eyes again.

"So, are you going to tell me who she is?" Hailey asked, caught completely off guard by Abby's reaction. Abby was suddenly not the calm, cool, overly confident woman she had known. She was someone else entirely. She looked sad, distant and withdrawn almost as if she was only a shadow of herself.

"Abby?" she asked again after she got no reply.

"What? Sorry. Did you ask me something?" Abby said suddenly coming back to the present.

"I asked who Erin was."

"No one," Abby replied curtly.

"Now, I know you're lying. Abs. Talk to me," Hailey pleaded, knowing they hid nothing from each other.

"She's just a woman I met in L.A." Abby replied hoping Hailey would just let it go, but at the same time, hoping she would ask to know more. Abby longed to talk to someone about Erin, but she didn't understand it herself so how could anyone else.

"She's the one you were thinking about that night. It really wasn't Lauren, it was Erin?" Hailey accused.

Abby nodded yes and looked deeply into Hailey's compassionate and questioning eyes for a glimpse of understanding. Seeing nothing of the sort she placed the napkin safely back in her briefcase and blankly asked, "Did you find that Carlysle data?"

Hailey smiled softly, understanding that Abby no longer wanted to discuss the woman in L.A. and held the file up for her to see. She paused for a moment hoping Abby would say something and when she didn't she returned to her own office file in hand.

Abby was all business the rest of the day as they worked steadily, knocking off one project at a time until they were nearly back on schedule.

"Do you mind if I invite some friends over for dinner?" Meg asked.

"No, I don't mind, but I'm not entertaining your friends, Megan," Erin replied.

"Well, just one is my friend, the other is her mother. Her mother who has recently broke up with her girlfriend," Meg said fearfully to her aunt who had still not gone out on a date since she moved in.

"NO WAY!" Erin shouted. "I will not have you set me up on some blind date."

"It's kind of too late. I already invited them. Would it really kill you to sit through dinner?"

"Kill me? No, it wouldn't kill me, but it might just cause me to start looking for a new roommate," she said seriously, making it clear to Meg that she would not tolerate this type of behaviour.

"Get real, Aunt Erin! It could be fun. You never know, you might actually like her. She's always very nice to me when I stop by."

"Nice? I'm sure she is. That doesn't mean I'll enjoy her company."

"Well, you'll know soon enough, they'll be here in a couple of hours," she said smiling nervously as she quickly stepped out of arm's reach of her aunt

"Tonight! You invited them over tonight. Why didn't you tell me earlier?"

"If I had told you, you would have found a way to get out of it. Now you have no choice but to hurry up and get ready."

"You little shit!" she screamed. "We'll discuss this some more later. Right now, I expect you to get the place cleaned up and make dinner for your guests," she said as she hurried into the bathroom to get ready.

"You're not wearing that!" Meg said as Erin appeared from the bathroom a while later wearing old torn blue jeans and a sleeveless Cal State sweatshirt.

"Why not?" Erin asked knowing that she had never intended on wearing this, but only put it on to torment her niece.

"Because, you look like you're about to go out and do some yard work or something. No wonder you haven't got a girlfriend," she replied, walking into her aunt's bedroom and rummaging through her clothes. "Here," she said handing her aunt a pair of jeans that were at least presentable, "wear these." She continued to rummage, "And this," she said as she handed her a black denim shirt.

"Are you sure? About the shirt, I mean," she said insecurely to Meg.

"Yes. It makes you look dark and mysterious; which you are, but for all the wrong reasons."

"Dark and mysterious? What am I a vampire?"

"Well, you might as well be the way you hide up here in your little cave all day," Meg said knowingly.

It was true. Erin rarely stepped foot outside anymore. She had no reason to. She couldn't really be angry with Meg because she was only trying to help, but she too, just like the rest of her family, interfered a little too much. As she got dressed in the clothes Meg had chosen for her, she grew increasingly anxious. She knew nothing of the woman she was about to meet except that her name was Joanne and that she had been through a bad break-up about three months ago. Meg had met her daughter, Stephanie, the week she moved in at some college orientation event and they had become instant best friends.

"I'll get it!" Meg shouted as she stood to answer the knock at the door.

"Hey Meg," Stephanie said, walking through the door with her mother following behind.

"Hey Steph! Hey Ms. Sanders!" she replied ushering the two women into the living room.

"How many times do I have to tell you to call me Joanne? Ms. Sanders makes me sound so old," she joked with Meg.

"Sorry, Joanne. I'll try to remember. Aunt Erin will be out in a couple of minutes. You guys want something to drink? Wine? Beer?"

"Wine would be good," Stephanie suggested, receiving a disapproving look from her mother.

"Stephanie, must I remind you, that you are not of legal drinking age?"

"Come on, Mom, it's not like I haven't had a drink before. Besides, I'm right here under your supervision," she whined.

"Oh, all right," she answered unable to rationally deny her daughter's request. "But just one glass," she added in a disciplinary tone.

Erin made her way from the bedroom dressed in the clothes Meg had picked out for her to find the three of them sitting in the living room talking and laughing. The sight was almost unnerving. She was the outsider in her own home. Meg had clearly spent a lot of time with both women and seemed very comfortable with them.

"Hi, I'm Erin," she said shyly as she entered the room.

Joanne immediately stood to greet Erin and tried to contain her excitement at first sight of her. Erin's strong features and warm smile were very intriguing.

"I'm Joanne, and this is my daughter, Stephanie," she said, extending her arm to meet Erin's waiting hand.

"Nice to meet you both," Erin said releasing her hand and taking the time to look carefully at the two women who seemed so similar yet so different. Joanne was exquisitely feminine. She was tall, maybe an inch or so taller than Erin's five-nine frame. Her long blond hair flowed naturally around her soft features. Her large breasts were shielded by a tight sweater, which accentuated her thin waist and womanly hips. She wore tight black jeans that showed off her long slender legs. Erin found it hard to believe that she was old enough to have an eighteen-year-old daughter. The woman had an air of power and professionalism about her that suggested success. Erin found parts of herself, which had long been dormant, suddenly awakening in response to the charming woman.

Diverting her attention, only for a moment, to study Stephanie, she found her to be every bit as attractive as her mother, but in a much more subtle way. They shared the same features and build, but where Joanne's hands had been perfectly manicured, Stephanie's were not. They seemed a bit rough to the touch, perhaps as a result of participating in some type of sport or perhaps from working with her hands. Joanne wore makeup, not too much, but Stephanie did not. She wore baggy blue jeans and a white t-shirt; very similar to what Erin, herself would wear. Immediately, Erin's gaydar sounded and she wondered if Meg knew that Stephanie was also a lesbian. Not that it mattered, she reminded herself of her friendship with Frankie. Although occasionally awkward when her body unknowingly responded to her friend's innocent touch, it was manageable.

"I must say, I was quite surprised with the invitation to dinner. Word on the street is that you are unattainable," Joanne said smiling seductively at Erin.

"Word on the street is sometimes inaccurate," Erin replied with a shy grin.

"That's good to know," Joanne responded innocently.

"Is there anything else they say about me?" Erin asked inquisitively as Meg and Stephanie watched the exchange in awe.

"Yes, but nothing I dare repeat in front of the children," she replied blushing with an unmistakable darkness appearing in her light green eyes.

"Like I said, word on the street is *sometimes* inaccurate," Erin replied. She had not intended on flirting with this woman, but somehow it felt good, her senses were waking up, her confidence renewed.

"Maybe I'll get the chance to find out?" She hinted, her eyes narrowing on Erin's lips.

Suddenly aroused and feeling a bit uncomfortable, Erin took a step back and said, "We should probably eat before it gets cold."

The four of them sat at the dining room table and talked freely and easily over the delicious pasta Meg had prepared. Gone now where the sexual overtones of their initial greeting and it became a relaxed and enjoyable dinner.

"So Joanne, what do you do for a living?" Erin asked as she cleared the last of their dinner plates from the table.

"I'm a real estate agent," she replied while refilling their wine glasses.

"Residential or commercial?" she asked, thinking that if nothing more, Joanne may be able to work with her on finding a new location for the club.

"I dabble in commercial, but I focus mostly on residential. Why do you ask?"

"Just something I might be planning soon that you may be able to help me with," she replied with a hint of secrecy. She had not discussed her plans with Meg yet and although her decision would likely not affect her at all, she'd hate for her to think she was keeping secrets.

"Perhaps we can discuss it over dinner one night," she smiled. "Just the two of us," she added with a wink and a hint of seduction in her voice.

"Perhaps we can," she answered, fighting back the urge to pursue this little game of flirtation between them.

'Mom, we should probably get going. I have to get up early tomorrow," Stephanie said while glancing at her watch, which now read ten-thirty.

"Okay Steph. Why don't you go wait downstairs for me? I'll be there in a minute."

Stephanie took the less than subtle hint and motioned for Meg to follow her downstairs so the two older women could have a moment alone. Joanne rose from her chair and gingerly headed for the door hoping Erin would follow and when she did, she lingered at the door with her hand on the handle for a brief moment before speaking.

"So, about that dinner we discussed?"

"I have to work every night this week. If you want to stop by, I'll buy you a drink and we could discuss the details of dinner then," she replied, completely aware that Joanne's lingering had little to do with asking about dinner and everything to do with the possibility of a goodnight kiss.

"Maybe I will," she responded and took the two necessary steps to close the distance between them and before she knew what was happening Erin's lips met hers for the first time. It was a soft, short kiss, but one that hinted of the possibility of more. Erin knew she had to stop, it had been so long since she had been touched that she feared she might lose control and usher this willing woman right to her bedroom.

"Stephanie is waiting for you. You had better go."

"I supposed I should, but I would rather keep doing this," she replied kissing Erin once again. This time the kiss was a little deeper, a little longer and Erin once again pulled away. She smiled softly. The woman couldn't possibly know that if she continued to kiss her like that she would find herself naked in bed before she knew what had happened.

"You really should go. Stephanie is waiting." She reiterated the fact that the woman's daughter would surely know what was taking her so long.

"Who?" she asked breathlessly as if mesmerized by the kiss.

"Your daughter. Stephanie," she repeated.

"Steph. Shit! I forgot. I had better go while I still can," she replied in a disappointed tone.

As she stepped through the door, she paused and said, "You know," she took a deep breath, "Some of what they say about you is *quite* accurate."

Erin closed the door behind her and stood looking around, her lips still tingling from the kiss. If it had not been for Meg, she would probably still be sitting here alone every night missing Dinah or thinking about Abby. Just then, Meg walked through the door and smiled at her knowingly.

"So, how was it?" she asked playfully.

"How was what?"

"The kiss."

"There was no kiss and even if there was I wouldn't be discussing it with you." She lied hoping Meg would believe her.

"If you didn't kiss her, why do you have that *just been kissed* look?"

Erin shook her head. There was no way she was ever going to be able to hide anything from her niece and she supposed it was time to get used to it.

"It was nice." She answered. She thought it was a safer answer than the truth, which was, it made me want to fuck her right there in the hallway.

Meg smiled, and Erin decided it was time to deflect the conversation to something a little more important and that was her friendship with Stephanie. "Meg, you know Steph's a lesbian too right?"

"No kidding, Aunt Erin! Do you think I didn't know that the minute I met her," she responded sarcastically.

"No, it's just that sometimes it can get complicated, that's all."

"Complicated; complicated like how you drool over Frankie all the time."

Erin smiled knowingly. "Yes, something like that. You just have to be careful about not leading her on. It's not so easy sometimes."

"I understand, I think. She wouldn't be interested in me anyway. You should see her girlfriend Chloe. She almost makes me want to switch teams. I swear she must spend six hours a day in the gym."

"I think, I'm quite sure I know what you mean," she replied knowingly, and just like that, the woman she had so successfully been able to stop thinking about for the first time in months was tormenting her again.

Meg was sure she saw her aunt's expression change from joy to lust to pain all within a fraction of a second. "I'm going to bed," Erin said soberly.

"What's wrong?" she asked, completely unaware of why her aunt's mood had shifted so suddenly.

"Nothing. You should go to bed too! You start your new job tomorrow." She waved a goodnight and closed her bedroom door behind her.

## Chapter Thirteen

Abby stopped by the grocery store on her way home from work to get a few things she desperately needed. She had done without many things lately simply out of pure laziness and the desire to be a recluse. She went to work but avoided all other public places. She no longer spent any time with Hailey outside of work.

Despite all of her efforts, she had been unable to stop thinking about Erin. She had gone so far as to look up her phone number, but every time she worked up the courage to dial it, she'd hang up before anyone answered. What would she say if someone did answer? Erin would probably be angry with her if she even remembered her at all.

It was hopeless and there was something else tugging at her emotions as well. She still hadn't gone to see her mother.

She quickly put away the groceries, packed an overnight bag and hopped into her car before she changed her mind.

As she drove up US-131 toward Big Rapids, her nerves began to get the better of her. What did she expect Helena to do when she showed up on her doorstep? Welcome her with open arms? Probably not. She had long ago forgiven her mother, but now she was ashamed of avoiding her this whole time. Maybe she wasn't even there. She should be though, considering she left Abby several messages over the last few months saying that she was at the cabin almost every weekend.

Abby was surprised at her ability to remember how to get to the cabin. A place she had so long ago forgotten even existed. As she pulled into the long, winding driveway, she knew she had the right place. The cabin was nestled in the woods and looked remarkably like a smaller version of her own home. It's no wonder that she had been instantly drawn to her house. Despite her father's objections at the time, Abby wanted that house and although she did not understand why until just now, she had never regretted the decision.

They must have heard her pull up to the house because when she did, in the near darkness, she could see the shadow of a man walking towards her from the rear of the house. It was Bill and he didn't seem at all surprised to see Abby this time. "Hello Abigail," he said cheerfully when she stepped out of the car and approached him. "I thought you might stop in soon."

"Hello, Mr. Morris." She greeted him warmly, but formally, because of her own insecurities this time. She knew she had been rather rude to him when they last spoke, but she was angry then. Now, she only wanted forgiveness and understanding. "I know it's late. I'm sorry if I'm interrupting anything," she added hesitantly. Perhaps they had guests. Perhaps her mother wasn't even here with him.

"Nonsense, Abigail. The night is young. Your mother is around back, if you'd like to see her. In the mean time, can I get you a beer?" he asked nervously, still a bit unsure of the intention of Abby's visit. He had hoped she would come to reconcile with her mother, but he wasn't certain.

"That sounds wonderful. Thank you," she said sincerely, realizing for the first time, what a truly wonderful man her mother had married.

She slowly made her way around the side of the house to find her mother curled up in a big chair by the fire reading a book. She was so pre-occupied with her book that she didn't bother to look up to see who it was standing next to her. Assuming is was Bill, Helena casually said, "Hi Honey!"

Abby thought quickly of about a hundred different ways to announce herself and only one seemed to make sense that very moment. "Hi Mom!" she said softly as she crouched down next to her mother's chair. There was a long moment of silence as Helena reconciled in her head that her daughter was there and that she had called her Mom.

"Oh Abby!" she exclaimed tossing her book aside and wrapping her arms around her daughter. Tears flowing freely down her face. The sight of her mother crying was more than Abby could bear and she herself broke down and cried.

Several minutes later Bill reappeared with Abby's beer and interrupted them for a moment to hand it to her before returning to the confines of the house. They may well have stayed like that all night had he not interrupted them. He understood that they needed to cry, but they needed to talk. The crying could come later.

"I'm sorry, Mom." Abby was the first to speak. "I should have …"

"Shh! We both should have done a lot of things. But we didn't and none of it matters now. We can't change what has already happened."

"I suppose you're right." Abby hadn't thought about it, but maybe it was just best to leave the past behind and start over. The bad parts of the past anyway. There were some good parts she was sure she wanted to remember.

"Have you eaten dinner, dear?"

"Actually, no. I hadn't planned on coming up here tonight. I guess I forgot to eat dinner," she said shyly. Not only had she intruded on their quiet evening, now she was asking for food too.

"Bill, honey!" she shouted toward the house.

"Yes, dear!" he replied appearing from the house with another beer for Abby.

"Would you mind heating up some leftovers for Abby? She hasn't eaten dinner yet."

"That's not necessary, really. I can ..." she started to say but was interrupted again by Bill, who insisted she sit and talk with her mother, while he prepared something for her to eat.

"He's amazing, Mom. I can see why you married him."

"He is, isn't he," she said with a sigh of gratitude. "What about you, Abby? Are you still seeing Lauren?"

"No. I've managed to avoid getting involved with anyone. It's easier that way."

"I'm sorry to hear that. I always hoped you'd find someone special. I don't know what I'd do without Bill. It's like I was incomplete until I found him."

"I don't think I'm meant to fall in love. It all seems so foreign to me."

"You'll know it when it happens, Abigail. When you find that special person, you'll feel it. It will happen when you least expect it and there won't be any rhyme or reason to it."

"Is that how it was for you?"

"The day I met Bill, my life changed. I felt so different when I was around him. I knew almost immediately that we were meant to be together."

"You knew, but you still waited to be with him?"

"Sometimes you have to make difficult choices. At the time, you were my priority and Bill understood that."

"Thank you."

"You don't have to thank me, Abigail. I'm your mother; that's what mother's do. The greatest gift you can give me is to find your own happiness. Maybe you should stay here for a few days and clear your mind. It might do you some good. It will give you time to figure out who you really are and where you're headed."

Abby took her mother's advice and spent the whole week at the cabin. She spent a lot of time soul searching. She looked forward to meeting her new half-brother and sister soon. Joshua was ten and in the sixth grade; Nicole was five. Her mother told them just recently that they had a half-sister named Abby, and she said they were looking forward to meeting her when they got out of school in a few weeks.

It was nice to have a family to share things with. Both the good and the bad. As much as she loved her father and saw him every day, he wasn't much of the sharing kind and neither was she, at least until now.

Erin's anxiety increased as they pulled into the driveway. It had been over six months since she left, but somehow, it felt like it was just yesterday. The memories of her girlfriend and her best friend in bed together were vivid and she nearly decided to turn around and go back, but Meg insisted she stay.

"You need to do this, Aunt Erin. If you don't, you'll never move on. It's time. And besides that, you want your bike back don't you?"

For a young woman, Meg was wise beyond her years and Erin was blessed to have her around. As they approached the front door Erin remarked on how rundown the house looked. The grey, three-bedroom ranch, which once sparkled and smelled of fresh flowers now looked dismal, nearly abandoned. The flowers Erin had painstakingly planted and cared for were dead. The little bit of grass that remained was overgrown. The paint on the windows and doors was dull and cracked.

Dinah answered the door clad in little more than a bikini and it was clear she had been drinking. She was thin—too thin. She smelled of alcohol and tobacco and looked as if she had been sleeping. "Your stuff is in the garage," she said as she picked up a long t-shirt and pulled it over her body.

"Where's Carly?" Erin asked as they walked to the garage at the side of the house.

"She moved out a couple of weeks ago," Dinah said sadly.

"Oh," was all Erin could say. Although she was curious, she really didn't care to ask. The sooner she could get out of there, the better. Since Dinah and Carly had packed all of Erin's things up long ago, there was little to do except load the boxes into the car. As they did, they did not speak.

"Meg, would you mind giving us a little privacy for a few minutes?" Dinah said after helping to load the last of Erin's belongings into the car.

Meg looked at her aunt hesitantly, wondering if she should just stay in case something happened. Dinah didn't look stable. She wasn't at all comfortable with the notion of leaving the two of them alone.

"Go ahead Meg, take the car home. I won't be far behind you," Erin said in a reassuring voice.

Meg did as she was told, and as soon as she was out of earshot, Dinah stepped closer to Erin and began to speak. "I've missed you so much, Erin," She whispered into her ear. "Take me for a ride."

"I don't think so," Erin replied curtly.

"Why not?" she asked. "Don't you remember the fun we had together? Don't you remember my hard nipples pressed against your back; my hot breath on your neck, like this," she said as she moved behind Erin and wrapped her arms around her waist pushing her breasts firmly against her back, her hot breath teasing at her neck.

Erin trembled. "I remember," she said shakily, her head swimming with memories she had long ago forgotten. They had had some good times together, some wonderfully passionate times together. On occasion, they'd pull off to the side of the road, make their way into the dense brush, and make love for hours. The first two years of their relationship had indeed been passionate and spontaneous. But that part, the passionate part, had been lost long before they broke up.

Dinah felt her tremble and walked around to face her. She caught and held Erin's eyes and pleaded once again. "Take me for a ride"

Erin was lost for a moment in her amazingly blue eyes. Eyes, which had so many times captivated hers over the years. Tonight, however, she saw nothing. She suddenly felt cold and empty. Just to be sure, she cupped the back of Dinah's neck and pulled her into a hard kiss. Dinah moaned in response and Erin smiled into the kiss realizing that she felt absolutely nothing for this woman. She no longer loved her or hated her. She felt nothing.

"See baby, you missed me too. I knew you would," Dinah said misunderstanding the reason behind Erin's smile.

"No. I thought I missed you, but I don't."

"Then why did you kiss me?"

"Just to be sure," she replied and, as she said it, she climbed on her bike and drove off leaving Dinah standing in the driveway completely bewildered.

On the ride home, she felt freer than ever, her mind clearer than ever. She was finally ready to move on with her life. Joanne had stopped by the club the Thursday before, and they decided that their first official date would be on Tuesday. She was looking forward to spending a wonderful evening with the sensuous woman. The knowledge that Dinah was completely out of her system restored a vigour deep within her soul that caused her heart to beat a little stronger and a little faster than it had in a very long time.

Abby's week at the cabin had been an emotional one. Between reconciling with her mother and putting her life into perspective, Abby felt drained, both emotionally and physically. She spent a lot of time over the week trying to identify exactly what she wanted. What she had been missing in her life? Could she really ever love someone the way her mother had explained it? Could Erin be that special someone her mother referred to? It couldn't be possible could it? It seemed extremely unlikely. She didn't know Erin except for that little bit they discussed at dinner that night; hardly enough to cause her to fall in love. Maybe this strange attraction toward her was nothing more than her desire to finish what they had started that night. Perhaps if they had had sex, she would have been able to walk away.

She needed to lose herself for a few hours and knew exactly who could help her do that. Two hours later, she found herself knocking on Hailey's door.

"Well, well. Look who's here. Where have you been hiding, Abigail?"

Abby didn't answer her. She didn't have to. When Hailey looked into Abby's eyes, she knew why she was there.

"Come here," Hailey said holding out her arms to draw Abby into a warm embrace. Hailey knew only one way to comfort Abby so she hopped into her arms and said, "Take me to bed."

Abby was a little bit shocked at Hailey's directive, but wasted no time manoeuvring her way to the bedroom. There was a newfound tenderness to their lovemaking this time and Abby found herself wondering how Hailey knew what she needed at that moment. Their previous encounters had always been goal oriented, but this time was different. It was tender and slow and Abby quickly let go of her pain and her barriers and simply let Hailey love her and comfort her.

"You okay, Abs?" Hailey asked as she gently caressed Abby's face.

"Yeah. Thank you. It amazes me that you always seem to know what I need." Abby confessed. It was true, for some reason Hailey was willing to put up with Abby and all the baggage that went along with her. She could never have asked for a better friend.

"You ready to talk about it?"

"Maybe later," Abby replied, allowing a mischievous grin to appear on her face. "I'd rather do more of this, right now," she added as she roughly, but playfully pinned Hailey to the bed.

A few hours later, both women lay there completely exhausted. It was well after 2:00 AM and Abby would normally have left a long time ago leaving Hailey cold and alone in her bed. Tonight though, to Hailey's surprise, Abby made no attempt to leave. She simply wrapped her strong arms around Hailey and softly whispered, "Goodnight."

For reasons unknown to either of them, they both knew this would be their last night together.

The next morning, Abby was ready to talk. She asked Hailey what she thought it felt like to be in love. When Hailey replied with almost the exact same assessment as her mother, Abby finally brought up the topic of Erin.

"Do you believe in love at first sight?"

"I think it's very rare, but I think it happens."

"Remember that cocktail napkin you found … Erin, the woman from L.A.?"

"You finally ready to tell me what really happened?"

Abby told Hailey the whole story. She had gone over the entire episode so many times in her head that it was easy to reiterate it to Hailey nearly word for word.

"I can't stop thinking about her. I've tried. I just can't forget about her. Do you think it's just because I didn't have sex with her?" Abby asked, hoping the answer was affirmative. That would be so much easier to deal with.

"That depends. When you fantasize about her, are your fantasies mostly sexual?"

"No. Mostly they're just about us being together. When I wake up in the morning, I wish that she was there next to me. Why is this happening to me? I just want to forget I ever met her."

"Wow Abs. I think maybe your feelings for her are real. Do you think she feels the same way? You know how to get in touch with her; why don't you call her?"

"I'm sure she must hate me. I walked out and didn't even have the decency to leave a note. She's probably forgotten all about me by now. What am I supposed to do call her and say 'Hi, it's Abby, do you remember me? The woman who snuck out of your bed at four in the morning and didn't call you or leave a note?'" she sighed. "That's not likely to go well Hailey. I just have to find a way to move on. Maybe I need to meet someone new."

## Chapter Fourteen

Erin was nervous. She hadn't been on a date in a long time. She was so out of practice, it terrified her. She decided to call on an old friend for a favour. Diane was one of her oldest and dearest friends and she owned a gay-friendly restaurant on the beach. Oceans, was a steak and seafood restaurant that had an unusual atmosphere that screamed of casual elegance. She had arranged with Diane to have her favourite table available and requested fresh flowers. She knew exactly what time to make the reservation for so that they would just be finishing their meals when the sun went down.

When Joanne answered the door, Erin immediately lost her calm, cool demeanour and stood awestruck staring at the woman. She was dressed head to toe in tight black leather. Her low cut jacket zipped up just high enough to ensure nothing would fall out, but still low enough to reveal her beautifully bronzed cleavage and a hint of black lace that seemingly was the only other thing enveloping her voluptuous breasts.

"Like what you see?" she said seductively to the still speechless woman who had not yet taken a step into the house. "Erin?" she smiled sweetly. "Are you okay?"

"Hmm? What? Sorry ... I ..." She was trying to focus, but was having a difficult time. *Say something, anything coherent,* she said to herself. "You look amazing." She had hoped to come up with something a little more original, but at least it was a coherent thought.

"I thought you might like it. Are you going to stand out there all night?" she added teasingly. Clearly, she was having the desired effect on Erin, but perhaps it was a little too much. She wasn't going to get what she wanted if the woman couldn't even function around her. She decided to leave her standing at the door and head into the kitchen so that she could gather her thoughts.

After she was gone a few seconds, Erin was able to think again. Relax. You can do this. She's just a beautiful woman. A beautiful woman, who in a few minutes will have her arms wrapped around you, holding on tight. She suddenly wished she had decided to take the car, but Joanne loved motorcycles, and Erin had always found a romantic ride to be a wonderful interlude to sex. She shook her head and finally stepped into the house finding Joanne in the kitchen. Thankfully, she had zipped her jacket up a little higher. "Ready to go?" she asked in a nonchalant voice that surprised even herself.

Joanne nodded and a minute later, they were on the road headed towards the coast. Erin found it surprisingly easy to focus on driving. Joanne was clearly an experienced rider so she was barely holding on and she made a point of not allowing her hands to travel even though she wanted nothing more than to explore Erin's body.

Diane had the table prepared as requested and had gone the extra step of ensuring there were no occupied tables anywhere near them. *Diane, I owe you big time.* They were seated very close to each other in perpendicular fashion and Erin's heart nearly stopped each time the woman seated next to her innocently, or maybe not so innocently, touched her. Once their drinks arrived, she started to regain her composure. Whether it was the alcohol or the fact that she was in familiar surroundings, she was quickly getting back to her old self. She needed to regain control of this situation and become the one doing the seducing.

After they ordered their meals, she reached over, softly brushed her fingers over the back of Joanne's hand, and was pleased to see the other woman's reaction. It was a simple touch, but it was enough to get a slight moan from Joanne. Their eyes met and Erin could see nothing but desire. She had to kiss her. The urge was overpowering. Joanne's lower lip quivered as Erin ran her index finger from the base of her earlobe down her jaw line to her chin. Once there, she used the finger, now resting beneath Joanne's chin, to pull her gently forward into a kiss. Their lips met so softly at first it was as if they hadn't touched yet. Joanne moaned again, raising Erin's state of arousal. "We should stop this before we cause a scene?" she said as she pulled away to catch her breath.

"Okay, I'll stop, but only if you promise we can continue this later."

"I promise," Erin replied eagerly.

Their food arrived and Joanne began to tell Erin about the properties she had located for her to look at. "We could probably see all four of them in one day. When would be good for you?"

"How's Sunday? I would like to bring Meg along too, if you don't mind."

"Sunday it is then."

Just as planned, the sun began to set as their dinner plates were being cleared. It was a beautiful spectacle of colours. Pinks, oranges and purples. The sunset was reflecting off of Joanne's eyes and Erin was sure she had never seen such a sight before. She wasn't sure which was more beautiful, Joanne or the sunset. "You are breathtakingly beautiful," she whispered softly.

"Are you always this romantic?" Joanne asked looking deeply into Erin's eyes.

"I try."

Erin was just about to kiss Joanne again when a familiar figure caught her eye. It was Lauren. Seeing Lauren filled her mind with memories of Abby. What would have happened if she hadn't told Abby to go dance with Lauren that night? Would Erin have seen Abby again? Would anything have been different? She tried to show at least some interest in what Joanne was saying, but she was extremely distracted; all she could think about was Abby and her strong, loving arms.

"Are you okay?" Joanne asked as they stood in her driveway. "You've been awfully distant since dinner."

Erin leaned back, kind of half sitting against her bike and looked at the beautiful woman standing a mere foot away from her and wondered why she couldn't keep her mind off of Abby.

"I'm sorry. I'm just a little bit distracted." That was an understatement. On the ride home, Joanne had gotten a little braver and had slipped her hand inside Erin's jacket and had teasingly stroked her abdomen and then wandered down between her thighs. Although her body reacted as it should. Her mind was somewhere else entirely.

"Distracted huh? Well, let's see what I can do about that?" she said as she stepped between Erin's legs and leaned forward to meet her lips. Erin was temporarily lost in the kiss. Her body was currently winning the fight between mind and body. She put her hand gently around Joanne's throat and slowly lowered it down the woman's body, unzipping her leather jacket in the process. Her hands trembled as they slid inside the jacket and cupped the bountiful breasts eliciting a low moan from Joanne.

Suddenly, her mind betrayed her again and she pulled away.

"What is it with you?" Joanne asked impatiently.

*God I wish I knew.* "I'm sorry. I just can't do this."

Joanne stepped back and lifted Erin's face so that their eyes met. She looked deeply into her eyes for the truth and found what she was looking for. "Someone's got a hold of you right here," she said as she placed her hand over Erin's heart. "Someone you can't have, but you can't let go."

Erin was speechless. Was she that easy to read?

"Listen. I don't intend on giving up on this, so when you're ready, you know where to find me. In the mean time," she zipped up her jacket and kissed Erin softly on the lips, "I will look forward to seeing you on Sunday."

Erin made her way home in a daze. Abby obviously wasn't all that interested in her or she wouldn't have snuck out in the middle of the night. This was insanity. It had to stop. Somehow, someway, she had to let this go. But how? If Joanne wasn't enough to take her mind off of Abby, who the hell could? Maybe the distraction of opening the new bar would help. She could occupy herself with work for a couple of months. That would certainly help. *Hopefully.*

Abby was feeling much better. Her weekend with Hailey had been therapeutic in so many ways and as the week progressed, she was feeling more and more like her old self. She and Hailey had decided that they should go out tonight and Abby was excited at the prospect of meeting someone new. It had been so long since she'd been out just to have fun that she was also a little bit nervous. She hadn't gone out since her trip to L.A. several months ago. Tonight would be exactly what she needed. She relished the idea of being her old self again. She was an expert at the game of seek and conquer and she was looking forward to finding someone new to play with.

Her thoughts were suddenly interrupted by the receptionist's voice on the intercom. "Your eleven o'clock is here, Abby."

"Thanks. Send her in and please ask Hailey to join us."

A few minutes later Toni Saroli stood in the doorway of Abby's office. She was the district sales rep for the engineering software CG Designs used. She routinely stopped by to update Abby on the latest software developments. She was sexy as hell and made it no secret that she would be interested in a relationship with Abby. Abby, of course, wanted no part of that for many reasons, not the least of which was her disdain for the sales profession. If she could talk her into buying software she didn't need, what else could she talk her into? But damn, she was sexy, dressed exquisitely as usual, in a perfectly tailored black pant suit with a very revealing low cut white ruffled blouse. Her long blond hair was pulled back into a perfect ponytail accented with a gold clip. She was about Abby's height, but her mere presence commanded attention no matter where she was. Men and women alike ogled her and she had often been the subject of Abby's fantasies. Her features were soft, but there was a hidden mischievousness about her hazel eyes that made her almost dangerous.

"Hello Toni," Abby said as she stood to greet her.

"Abby. You're looking well as always," she said with a hint of seduction in the tone of her voice as she took Abby's hand and kissed her softly on the cheek.

"Abs, you asked for me?" Hailey said as she entered Abby's office head down reading a file. She was completely unaware of the other woman's presence until Abby spoke.

"Hailey, I'd like you to meet Toni Saroli. She's the sales rep for KJP and I'd like you to start getting more involved in these types of decisions."

The two women stared at each other as if Abby was not even in the room. She expected this from Hailey, but not from Toni. It was clear that there was instantly an attraction between them. She looked back and fourth from one to the other and could not believe that the unflappable Toni Saroli stood there with her mouth hanging open like an awestruck teenager. She cleared her throat loudly, hoping to break the spell. Suddenly, Toni regained her composure and extended her hand to Hailey. "It's a pleasure to meet you, Hailey."

Hailey shook her hand gently, but firmly, and was surprised at just how soft the woman's hands were. *Nobody's hands are that soft.* She wondered exactly how soft the rest of her body was. "The pleasure is all mine, I assure you."

*You have to be kidding me. She's actually falling for that line of crap. Jesus Hailey! You certainly have something a little more creative in that brain of yours.* But it appeared as though Hailey could have punched her in the face and elicited a welcome response from this woman who was flushed and breathing a little heavier than when she had walked in. After what seemed like an endless amount of time, Hailey finally released Toni's hand and gallantly pulled out a chair for her.

As Toni pitched the latest piece of software her gaze remained fixed on Hailey. *Hey! You're supposed to be selling this shit to me not her.* She let it go. Maybe Hailey had a chance for something special with Toni. Who was she to stand in the way? Abby ignored the rest of Toni's well-rehearsed proposal and let her mind wander as she gazed hopelessly out the window. Why couldn't she find someone who would have that effect on her?

"Would you ladies like to join me for lunch?" Toni asked as she stood and placed a folder of information on Abby's desk for her review.

"I'm actually not very hungry. Why don't the two of you go?" she suggested, wanting no part of what was no doubt going to be nauseatingly absurd to watch.

"Okay then. Hailey, will you join me for lunch?" She could barely contain her smile when Abby opted out of lunch leaving just herself and Hailey.

"It would be an honour to accompany you to lunch."

*Okay this had to stop. I can't believe it's working.* Part of her wanted to shake the hell out of Hailey and tell her just to be herself; another part of her wanted to shake the hell out of Toni and ask her if she could actually hear any of the absurdities coming out of Hailey's mouth. An entirely different part of her found this whole exchange to be just a little bit adorable. "You ladies have fun now!" she shouted as they left her office quickly.

"Hey Abs! Just give me a second!" Hailey shouted from the bedroom as Abby let herself into the apartment with the key Hailey had given her the weekend before. "I hope you don't mind, but Toni will be meeting us at the bar later on."

Abby smiled. She didn't mind. She didn't plan to spend much time there anyhow. "What do you think of her?"

"She's amazing. I've never met anyone like her," Hailey replied stepping into the living room looking absolutely adorable. She was wearing faded blue jeans and a black blouse that she didn't bother to tuck in. It was the expression of excitement combined with sheer terror that Abby found nearly irresistible.

"I'm actually surprised you came back to work this afternoon. I thought you would have brought her here instead."

"It's not that I didn't want to. It's just ... well ... I really, really like her. I didn't want to give her the wrong impression. I think we should get to know each other first."

"Is that the way it's supposed to work?" Abby replied sarcastically. "No wonder I'm still single."

"I don't know how long I can wait. It's like every part of her just exudes sex appeal. And her hands are soooo soft," she added dreamily as she starred out the window completely oblivious to Abby's presence.

"Ready to go?"

Abby chose a table in the corner of the dark, smoke-filled room. Music blared, making any effort at conversation impossible. By the time Toni arrived, Abby had already consumed a few drinks and had scoped the room for possibilities. Once she was certain Hailey was in capable hands, she made her way toward a short brunette that had caught her eye.

She was sitting with a small group of woman who had left her company for the moment to dance. As she approached the table, the brunette looked up at her and smiled shyly. *Perfect.* She was extremely cute and extremely young looking. *Perfect.* "Hi. I'm Abby," she said as she offered her hand to the hesitant looking young woman.

"Jasmine," she replied nervously. *Perfect.*

"May I join you?" She didn't wait for a reply before taking a chair next to Jasmine.

It was much too loud for conversation so Abby did her best to convey her thoughts through her eyes and the occasional gentle touch of her fingers over the other woman's hand. She clearly seemed to be getting the message as she moved her chair closer to Abby's. Finally, a slow song began to play and the woman's friends returned. Abby instinctively stood and took Jasmine's hand and led her to the dance floor.

It was clear that they both had the same idea when Jasmine wrapped her arms around Abby's shoulders and nuzzled her face against her neck. Abby put her right hand on the small of her back and pulled her tightly against her enjoying the feeling of the young, hot, soft body against hers. The soft moan that escaped the young woman shot right through to Abby's core. Abby's left hand gently explored Jasmine's body. The firm hold of her right hand mixed with the gentle touch of her left hand were causing all sort of amazing sensations in Jasmine's body and her reaction was exactly what Abby was hoping for. "Do you want to get out of here?" she whispered into Abby's ear.

"Absolutely," she replied taking the time to stop by Hailey's table to say goodbye. "I'm sure you can ensure Hailey gets home safely?" she said to Toni before stepping away from the table.

"Where to?" Abby asked once they were seated securely in the car. Sensing a bit of anxiety from the woman in the passenger seat, Abby decided she had better do something before she changed her mind. She quickly released her seat belt and leaned over to capture Jasmine's lips tenderly. Initially, Jasmine seemed apprehensive, but the young woman quickly became a willing and very capable participant.

Abby was quickly losing control, and although she was notorious for one-night stands; having sex in the car was something she just didn't do. She needed room to manoeuvre, wanted the woman to be comfortable and didn't want the distraction of passer-by's. She finally made herself pull out of the kiss.

"Mmm. That was nice." Abby said. "Where do you want to go?"

"My place." She struggled to say through ragged breaths. "It's about twenty minutes away. Drive fast," she added as she stared out the window trying to regain her composure all the while giving Abby the directions.

After about ten minutes, the sexual desire somewhat subdued for the moment, Jasmine began to speak, and the more she did, the more Abby realized that she needed to extricate herself from this situation. She tried in vain to ignore the woman's constant babble about her friend's new shoes; how tired she was after her shift at the Burger King.... blah, blah, blah.

She used to be able to ignore this. Shut them out and just do what it was that she was there to do. Tonight however, she was incapable of ignoring it. Although she was very much attracted to Jasmine and her body was screaming for attention, she knew she wouldn't be able to go through with this. But why? Was it because she wanted to take Hailey's advice and get to know the woman first? Was it the face that she saw every time she closed her eyes? Whatever it was, she didn't like it. She had come here tonight to find her old self and thought she had, until now.

Once parked in the woman's driveway she looked into her expectant eyes and tried very carefully to avoid upsetting her "Jasmine, I'm sorry, I'm suddenly not feeling all that well. Maybe I had too much to drink or something. I have to go home and lie down. If you want I can take you back to Dreams on the way by?" She did her best to sound sincere and by the look on Jasmine's face, it was working.

"Are you sure? If you want, I can go with you and take care of you?"

"I'll be okay."

"I'm tired anyways. I guess I'll just stay here. Can I have your number? Maybe we could do this some other time?"

*Think fast Abby.* "I'm going to be moving in a couple of days, and I don't have my new number yet. Why don't you give me your number instead?"

"Don't you have a cell phone?"

"I did, but I lost it while I was packing. It's probably at the bottom of one of the boxes." *Good one, Abby.*

"Here's my number," she said as she handed Abby a piece of paper with her name and number on it. "It was nice meeting you. I hope you feel better."

Once she was safely inside the house, Abby pulled out of the driveway and made her way back to the interstate to head back home. She quickly tossed the piece of paper out the window. *Well, that was a disaster.* She needed to find a different way to meet women because she needed to meet a completely different kind of woman. No more of the ditzy, young bimbos. She needed to find someone with a brain. Someone who would challenge her. Someone like ... Erin.

# Chapter Fifteen

"I'd like to see the first one again, if it's not too much trouble," Erin asked as they exited the fourth of the properties Joanne had shown her.

"I thought you might. That's why I showed it to you first."

They made their way back to the first building. It was a single floor. An old brick warehouse that had been vacant for years. It didn't look like much in its current state, but it had a certain rustic charm to it that was undeniable and the structure was sound. Since it was a warehouse, there was little inside, mostly empty space, which would be perfect for what Erin had in mind. It also didn't hurt that it was only three blocks from her current location. She would have little trouble overseeing the construction while taking care of things at ED's.

"What do you think Meg?"

She looked at her aunt inquisitively, and then looked around the space. When she looked around she didn't see empty space, she saw tables and chairs and pool tables and televisions mounted to the walls. She saw a dance floor, mirrors and women. "I think it's perfect."

"Good. Joanne, I'll call you tomorrow with the details of my offer and to discuss the listing on the current building." Money would not be an obstacle since she had more than enough, but the last thing she wanted was to be a landlord. She had received a healthy settlement after being hit by a drunk driver when she was eighteen. He was a very influential politician who paid her well to keep his name a secret. Although she had been unconscious for several days, most of her injuries had been relatively minor. As part of the agreement, he paid all of her hospital bills, including the cost of the best plastic surgeon in town. Thankfully, she had no visible scars to remind her. The only thing she had was the money, which haunted her often. She had invested it immediately and used only what she needed to buy ED's which had since tripled in value.

"Why don't we make it Tuesday night? I'll take you to dinner?" she asked still not giving up on the possibility of continuing what they had started the week before.

"Okay. Six o'clock?" she suggested, still feeling a little bit uncomfortable being around Joanne since the debacle the other night, but Joanne didn't seem the least bit affected by it. She had even been flirting with her most of the day despite Meg's presence.

Abby was waiting impatiently in her office. She couldn't sleep so she went into the office at 5:00 AM and was waiting for Hailey who wouldn't arrive for at least three hours. She had spent the rest of her weekend up at the cabin with her Mom and Bill getting to know her half-brother and half-sister. It had been a wonderful experience.

Since the cabin only had three bedrooms, she was certain she would be sleeping on the couch, but when she arrived, Bill asked her to help him assemble the new bunk bed he purchased the day before. He thought Abby would be more comfortable in her own room when she stayed there, especially if she ever wanted to bring someone along. She felt terrible that the kids would have to share a room, but they didn't seem to mind at all.

In the few hours she spent alone with Bill she couldn't help but realize how completely different he was from her father. He was a kind, caring, compassionate man, who seemed very involved in his children's lives. And more than that—he cherished her mother. Although she knew she shouldn't feel the way she did, she almost felt guilty that her mother had to be without Bill for all those years while she watched over her. It didn't seem fair, but she shouldn't feel guilty, she had no idea any of it was going on.

The memories of the weekend were causing an unusual, warm and fuzzy sensation to envelop Abby's body. She never realized that she even missed having family in her life and she was suddenly longing for the other things she didn't have in her life. Now, more than ever, she knew she had to find that someone special. She wanted to find someone to cherish the way Bill cherished her mother. How was she ever going to find that special person? The thought was overwhelming and she felt tears starting to well up in her eyes. Why couldn't she simply go back to her old self?

She was happy back then, or at least she thought she was. Now, she had all these emotions that she wasn't sure what to do with. Her old life was simple. There were no complications. She came and went as she pleased and went about her life without worrying what anyone thought of her. Now, she suddenly felt an obligation to make her mother proud—an obligation to be a good example for her new siblings—an obligation to be a good friend to Hailey—and more than anything else, an obligation to make herself happy. How could one trip to Los Angeles have caused all of these changes? The trip was the root of this entire transformation. The fact that she had let it all happen was very disconcerting. Thankfully, Hailey walked in to stop any further introspection.

"Hey Abs," she said sporting a huge grin.

"Hailey! How was your weekend?"

"Wonderful," she said dreamily. "I think I'm in love." She sighed remembering the wonderful time she'd had with Toni on the weekend. They had gone to dinner and a movie on Saturday and spent Sunday just sitting in a park down by the lake talking. It was so easy, so right. She was so lost in a daydream about how soft Toni's lips were and how much she wanted to do more than kiss her that she didn't hear Abby talking to her.

"HAILEY!" Abby shouted trying to get Hailey's attention.

"What? Sorry, I was lost in thought." She felt her face flush.

"Wow! You've really got it bad, haven't you?" Abby was surprised at how happy Hailey seemed. She was beaming. She wondered, sadly, if she would ever get to experience that feeling.

"Yeah, it's pretty bad. I haven't been able to do anything but think about her since last night." Toni had left around 7:00 PM because her work required her to travel the entire Southern half of the state. She had to leave so that she could be ready for a seven o'clock meeting the next morning near Detroit. Although only an hour and a half away, she'd be working in that area all week and probably wouldn't make it back to Lansing until Friday afternoon. Hailey missed her already. They had talked over the phone four times since then, but that did little to make the longing go away.

"How did things go after you left on Friday?" she asked, wanting to deflect the sudden discomfort she was feeling.

"I couldn't do it."

"You what?" Hailey asked as if unsure of what she'd just heard.

"I couldn't go through with it. I tried. I wanted to. Things were fine until she started talking. I just couldn't ignore it this time. She irritated the hell out of me."

"I thought that's the way you liked them. Young, gorgeous and brainless?" she accused wondering how she had ever gotten involved with Abby to begin with, since she was none of those things.

"I thought I did. But now ... I think I need more. I'd like to be able to carry on an intelligent conversation with someone. I'm finding myself wanting things I never knew I was even missing before and I don't know what to do about it."

"Sounds like you might finally be growing up."

"You think?" she said cocking her head slightly to the left. "The only thing I know is that nothing's been the same since my trip to L.A."

Erin sat quietly opposite Joanne who was chatting discreetly on her cell phone to a client. She was still uncomfortable in her presence. Had she been on the receiving end of that type of rejection she's certain she wouldn't have handled it quite so well. She would have been angry and bitter. Not Joanne, though, she was taking it all in stride. Although dressed more conservatively tonight in a beautifully tailored navy business suit, she made no attempt at hiding her intentions, by bringing Erin to the most romantic Italian restaurant in the area.

The cozy little table where they sat was conveniently located in an area that was somewhat secluded. The soft music, dim lighting and the golden flicker of candles were not completely lost on Erin who felt herself relaxing slightly and once again taking in the beautiful features of the woman across from her. Her body started to respond again as it had the week before—longing to be touched. She had an aching need that had been neglected for months.

She should be able to do this. She was an adult after all, but there was a deeper void—one in her heart. When Abby left her bed all those months ago, she had taken with her a piece of Erin's heart and no matter how much she reasoned with herself that she was not coming back, every night she kept an eye on the door hoping and praying for her to walk back in and make her whole again. She had never felt so safe as she had in Abby's arms, but the cruel reality was, that she was not safe at all—Abby was very, very dangerous and she had known it the minute she set eyes on her.

"Sorry about the interruption, but it's part of the job. Ironically, the after hours calls are usually more promising. They're impulse buyers and by the time they have time to really think about what they're doing, I've already shown them the property and they want it so bad they usually find a way."

"That's a little bit ruthless don't you think?"

"Maybe so, but it usually works," she licked her lips seductively. "Except on you."

Erin bit back a response as the temperature in the small room grew exponentially.

"I don't suppose you've changed your mind yet?" Her eyes, smouldering with desire, captured Erin's and her now shoeless foot rested intimately between Erin's thighs. Erin closed her eyes at the sensation. It felt so good. She wanted this so badly.

"I could try, but I'm afraid I might disappoint you again."

She withdrew her foot. "I don't think I could handle another rejection. I'll wait until you're sure." She sighed audibly. "But I refuse to quit trying.

Abby sat up abruptly from a sound sleep. She was sweating profusely and her heart was beating so fast she thought it might actually leap from her chest. *Damn.* She hadn't had that dream in months. She'd been running again, but this time it was different. The first few months after she got home from Los Angeles she'd had the same dream a few times a week, but thankfully the dreams had stopped—until tonight. The previous dream had always been the same; she was running from someone, but she could never quite make out who it was. It was as if she'd been running on a treadmill, because even if she ran faster and covered more distance; the dark shadow of the person she was running from never got further away.

Tonight's dream was just the opposite; she was running toward someone and no matter how fast she ran and no matter how close the figure seemed—she just couldn't reach it. Although the person's features were fuzzy and the facial detail was missing; she knew who she was running towards. It was Erin. *Fuck! Leave me alone! Why won't you go away?*

The bedside clock read 2:18 AM. Hailey would be busy with Toni. Her mother would be unreachable at the cabin. She needed to talk this out with someone and she realized sadly that there was no one. The realization wasn't a new one, but it was a lot clearer now. She had to make a change, and she had to do it soon before what little control she had left over her life and emotions was gone.

She made her way down to the kitchen took out a bottle of wine and dug out the phone book. Not bothering with a glass, she drank directly from the bottle while perusing the listings under the psychologist heading for potential choices. Her biggest prerequisite was that the doctor was a woman and that the office was close to work so that she could sneak out unnoticed. She could not admit to anyone, not even to Hailey, that she was going to see a psychologist because she couldn't get her life in order.

She jotted down three names and numbers that seemed like good possibilities and took what little was left of her bottle of wine up to bed with her.

Erin was growing ever more thankful for Joanne's company. They had continued to see each other frequently, but mercifully, Joanne had stopped trying to seduce her. As a result a wonderful friendship had developed.

Meg had been dating the same guy for about a month and things were starting to get serious. His name was Tom, he was a very attractive man, and although he seemed nice enough, Erin couldn't help but feel an underlying sense of mistrust. She chalked it up to simple jealousy because Meg was spending whatever little free time she had with him, leaving Erin alone again with way too much time on her hands.

"I've got an offer for you to look over," Joanne said as Erin opened the door and led her to the table.

"Tell me it's a good one." The offer she put on the new property would expire soon because of the condition that ED' be sold first. If it did expire, Erin knew she'd have to change her conditions and dip into her investments to pay for the property, but she didn't want to have the headache of dealing with two properties.

"I think it's a great offer. Just under asking price, but there is one condition." She paused to carefully re-read the offer to be certain of the details. "The buyer wants the loft to come with a tenant on a one year lease."

Surprised by the odd requirement, she looked over at Joanne inquisitively and asked "Why?"

"Really, it's more of an insurance thing. If there's a tenant, the building doesn't have to be insured as vacant during the renovations."

"What do you think I should do?" It seemed like a reasonable offer. She was also eager to get this over with so she could get started. She had met with architects and interior designers and had a vision of what the new club would look like. Her offer on the new property stipulated that she could begin renovations as soon as she had accepted an offer on her property, despite the fact that the ownership of the property would not transfer until the final payment was made.

"You know it would be irresponsible of me professionally to sway your decision one way or another."

"Forget professionally. Give me your personal opinion."

"Accept the offer," she said as she slid the paperwork over to Erin to sign.

Abby was startled awake by the sound of a ringing telephone. She quickly glanced at the clock noting with fear that it read 4:13 AM. She shook her head trying to wake up and forced herself to pick up the phone.

"Hello."

"Miss Grant?"

"Yes."

"My name is Jane. I'm calling from Lansing Memorial Hospital."

*Oh God! It must be Hailey.*

"Miss Grant? Are you still there?"

"Yes, sorry, please continue."

"Your father was brought in about an hour ago. He was in a car accident."

The words brought Abby to a state of full consciousness and her instincts took over. She was already getting dressed when she asked, "How is he?"

"I can't give you any details on his condition over the phone, but I suggest you come up to the hospital as soon as possible."

*Okay, so what you aren't telling me is that it's serious. Very serious.* She was remarkably calm considering the circumstances. "I'm on my way."

Half an hour later Abby was watching through a window in the hallway as the doctors worked frantically on her father. The nurse at the desk said his condition was serious and that they were trying to stabilize him so that they could run some tests to determine the extent of his injuries.

"Miss Grant?"

"Yes."

"I'm Dr. DiCarlo. I'm taking care of your father. He's stable now. We won't know the full extent of his injuries for several hours, but what we do know, is that he has two broken legs, he has some internal bleeding and a head injury."

Abby hoped she didn't look as pale as she felt. Her father was young and strong and she had never thought about what would happen if she lost him. She had just recently found her mother—how could she face losing her father now? "What are his chances?" she asked flatly trying to choke back the tears that were forming against her will.

"He's in good hands, Miss Grant. We're going to take him upstairs for a CT scan so that we can evaluate his head injury. Afterwards, we will take him to surgery to repair the internal damage. Until we get a chance to do those things, I can't say for certain what his chances are."

*Of course, you can. You know exactly what his chances are, but you won't tell me, you prick.*

"Can I see him?"

"Not right now, I'm afraid. We're going to move him immediately and all those people around him need to stay with him to keep him stable until we get him upstairs. You can see him right after the surgery."

"I understand." *No, I don't, but I don't have the wherewithal to argue with you right now.* "Is there someplace I can wait?" He guided her to a lounge, which looked as though it had not been redecorated since the seventies. The dim lighting, pea green walls and orange sofas had seen better days. The small TV in the corner of the room had been permanently stuck on CNN. It was only five-thirty in the morning. She couldn't call the office until at least eight o'clock. All she could do was wait. She tried to sit patiently, but that wasn't working, so she paced back and forth in the little ten by ten room, until someone appeared at the door with a cup of coffee.

"Miss Grant?" the attractive woman dressed in blue hospital scrubs asked with a gentle smile.

"Yes. Is there any news on my father?" she asked impatiently. She wasn't a patient person by nature so she was on her last nerve before the woman appeared.

"No. Not yet. Why don't you sit down? I brought you a cup of coffee," she said as she guided Abby back to the couch. "I'm Jane. I'm just finishing up my shift and I thought I'd check in on you before I left."

Abby looked at her appraisingly. She was an older woman, probably in her early fifties. She didn't wear a wedding band. Her long, dark hair, which was starting to show a hint of grey, was pulled back in a ponytail.

"Thanks for the coffee."

"You'll probably hear something soon. Is there anyone else we should call?" she asked as she made her way to the door to leave.

"No." Except for the office, there was no one for her to call. "Do you know if he was alone when the accident happened?" It suddenly occurred to her that perhaps he had been out on a date when the accident occurred and that maybe his date might be injured as well.

"When the police were here earlier they said that he was alone. A truck driver fell asleep and crossed the median into his path. That's about all I know. Sorry."

"Thanks again for the coffee," she said and gave a polite wave as the woman left the room.

Half an hour later Dr. DiCarlo appeared to give her an update. "The surgery went well. We removed his spleen and repaired some damage to his liver so we've controlled the bleeding for the time being. The CT scan showed evidence of a head trauma so we'll continue to monitor the swelling and if it doesn't respond to medication we may have to do surgery. He's stable right now, but his condition is still serious. We'll be moving him to his own room on the ICU floor in a couple hours and then you'll be able to see him."

"When will we know more? And what about his legs?"

"The next twenty-four hours are critical. Now that we have the internal bleeding under control, my biggest concern is the head injury. Once we have that under control, we'll work on his legs. He probably needs surgery on the right one because there are a few shattered bones."

"Thank you, Doctor. Please keep me informed."

It was nearly eight o'clock and she knew someone should be at the office. Ruth would certainly be there by now. She had been her father's first hire thirty years ago. She was discreet and efficient and despite her current age of sixty-one years old, she still worked a full day every day.

"Ruth, it's Abby."

"Good morning, Abby. Will you be late this morning? Do you need me to reschedule anything for you?"

"No Ruth!" she snapped, "I need you to listen to me." She had not meant to be so rude, but the stress and lack of sleep were definitely having an effect on her mood. "My Dad's been in a terrible accident. He's in the hospital."

"He's going to be okay though, right, Abby?"

"I don't know yet Ruth. I need you to clear his schedule at least for the foreseeable future. If there is anything critical that can't be handled by someone else I'll have to deal with once I know what's going on."

"Is there anything he needs? Can we visit him?" Ruth loved working for Carson. She respected him and often thought of him as a brother so Abby understood that Ruth would take the news rather poorly, but right now, she needed her to handle things at the office so she could concentrate her efforts here at the hospital.

"Ruth, I know you're worried. I'm worried too, but there's nothing any of us can do for him right now. I'll make sure to keep you informed, but it's important that you take care of the things I asked you to take care of."

"Okay Abby. I'll do my best. I just don't know what I'd do if ..."

"Ruth, don't talk like that. Think positively. Can you patch me through to Hailey please?"

She went through the whole story again with Hailey and asked her to stop by the house to pick up some clothes and whatever else she thought she needed for a few days since it appeared as though she wouldn't be leaving any time soon.

"Oh! Hailey, one more favour."

"Anything."

"Take care of Ruth. She's a basket case," Abby said with a hint of a smile.

"Will do. See you tonight."

# Chapter Sixteen

It had been three days since the accident and Abby had not left the hospital. How could she? He had no one else. As she sat there, she realized that, if she didn't soon find that special person in her life, she would probably end up lonely in a hospital bed just like him. Her visits with Dr. Bell had not been having the desired effect. She had hoped that after a few visits, she would feel better, but instead of answers, she had new questions. Dr. Bell had asked her if she thought her fear of relationships and love were a result of her father's example or a because of the way Mrs. Jones had treated her. If she knew the answer to that, she wouldn't have needed the Doctor at all. It was very frustrating. Wasn't the doctor supposed to be the one with the answers?

Jane was wonderful. She brought a cot for Abby to sleep on and always made sure she had eaten. Jane was spending an awful lot of time with them. Too much time. Whenever she had a break, she would peek in, and if Abby was sleeping, she would quietly sit by Carson's bedside. If Abby was awake, she would talk to her and reassure her.

Hailey and Ruth had things well under control at the office and she had managed to get in touch with her mother as a courtesy. The doctors were optimistic that her father would make a full recovery, but they were concerned that he had not regained consciousness yet.

Abby was resting peacefully in a chair when the sound of her father trying to speak startled her. It was about four in the afternoon and he hadn't moved at all since the accident. He looked broken and scared as Abby approached the bed. "Dad, do you know where you are?" She reached for his hand to offer him some reassurance.

"Hospital," he said roughly. He darted his eyes around the room stopping when he saw the pitcher of water on the table. "Water," he pleaded.

Abby poured him a cup of water and held the straw up to his lips. He grimaced in pain as he choked down the first few sips. Abby called for the nurse and left the room while they evaluated him.

She spent that one final night there at the hospital with him and then, due mostly to his insistence, went back to work, reducing her time there to about three hours a day. She would stop in on her way to work, spend her lunch hour with him and stop by once more on her way home. The doctors assured her that he would be fine, but that it would be several weeks, maybe even months, before he could go home.

She arrived at the hospital very early one day because she had a meeting first thing and was shocked to find Nurse Jane cuddled into her father on the bed. She turned to leave but Jane stopped her. "Wait Abby!" she whispered loudly as she grabbed her arm. "This isn't how it looks!"

"How do you think it looks?" Abby challenged. Why was this woman in her father's bed?

"Listen. Carson and I … um … we're old friends. We dated for a while about ten years ago."

"And?" she challenged again. *So, you slept with him a few times. Big deal.*

"Since he regained consciousness we've talked a lot. I'm going to be taking care of him when he leaves the hospital. He asked me to stay with him."

"I'm sure he did!" she said snidely. "I'm going to work. Tell him I'll see him at lunch time." It was fruitless to continue this conversation with her. She would have to discuss it with her father and he was still sleeping.

When she returned at lunchtime, her father had been ready to defend himself and wasted no time chastising her for her behaviour. "Abigail, how could you be so rude to Jane?"

"Dad, be honest with me, what's going on?"

"I never told you this, but not too long after your mother left, I met Jane. Even though I wouldn't admit it to myself back then, I fell in love with her and I've been running from that feeling ever since. Sitting in this hospital and seeing Jane again after all these years has put some perspective on what's important in life and Jane is important to me."

She couldn't believe what her father was telling her. All her life, he did nothing but discourage her from getting involved in a relationship. He taught her how to remain distant and avoid attachment and all along, he had kept Jane a secret.

"Don't get involved Abby! Protect your heart Abby! Isn't that what you always told me Dad?"

"I couldn't bear for you to be hurt, Abigail. I thought I was protecting you."

"How nice of you!" she said sarcastically. "How do you plan on protecting me from myself?" she asked angrily as she stammered out of the room.

"Hi Mr. Grant." Hailey said as she stepped through the door of his hospital room. It had been three weeks since the accident and he was recovering well, but it would still be a few more weeks before he was able to go home.

"Hailey! I'm glad you could get away for a little while." He had called a few hours earlier and asked Hailey to come up to the hospital because he had something important to discuss with her.

"Abby doesn't know you're here right?" he asked. Although Abby continued to visit him, she hadn't been very cordial since the day of their confrontation about Jane.

"No, Sir."

"Good. I need you to do me a favour."

"Anything, Sir."

"I need Abby to go to that trade show next week in Los Angeles. For some reason she refuses to go."

*I have a good idea why.* She doubted Abby would ever go back there. "What would you like me to do about that, Sir?"

"It's critical that she's there. There are some very important clients planning on attending that show and I need Abby there to convey to them that, despite my condition, their projects are on schedule and being handled effectively."

"I think that's going to be difficult to do. Isn't there someone else that can go?"

"Abby has to be there, Hailey!" His tone indicating that there was no point trying to negotiate any further. "Find a way to get her there. I don't care what it takes."

"I'll take care of it, Mr. Grant," she reassured him even though she had no idea how she was going to convince Abby to go back to the place that had upset the perfect balance of her life to the point that she has no idea who she was or what she wanted anymore. "Get well soon!"

"Abby, you're coming to L.A. with me," Hailey proclaimed with authority after marching into her office.

"Like hell I am. I've been in therapy twice a week for a month and a half and I'm finally starting to make progress," she lied, knowing that despite her best efforts, she still had more questions than answers as a result of her twice-weekly sessions with Dr. Bell. "I will not go back there for any reason."

"Don't you think it might help if you have some kind of closure?"

"What do you mean?"

"I mean, if she has moved on, and she is no longer available or if she hates you, at least you'll know for sure and then maybe you can let it go?"

Abby listened intently as Hailey explained herself. She had to admit it sounded as reasonable as anything else she's tried to rid her mind of Erin, but what if it had the opposite effect. It seemed too risky. "That seems too simple. What if it only makes it worse?"

"Honestly, Abs! Could it get any worse?" she knew it could, but she also knew she had to get Abby to go on this trip. "You never know, maybe she has feelings for you too?" *Doubt it. I'd hate her if she did that to me,* Hailey thought to herself.

"I hardly think that's possible. She could have tracked me down if that was the case."

"Yes, she could have. But you can't muster up enough courage to contact her so why should she be any different?"

*She's being very logical today, frustratingly so. How am I supposed to argue that?* Secretly, Abby had always kept a glimmer of hope that Erin did feel what she was feeling, but always pushed those thoughts quickly out of her mind. She was running out of arguments to support her decision not to go.

"Well that went extremely well!" Abby said as they entered the suite after meeting with the clients her father had insisted on her seeing at the trade show.

"No kidding! I thought for a minute they were going to bail, but you convinced them everything was fine."

"That's why I get paid the big bucks!" she said jokingly.

"Well, Miss Big Bucks, are you ready to tackle your next problem?" They decided that if Abby was going to sort out any of her feelings for Erin, it would have to be done while they could be alone before the club got too busy.

"I don't know that I'll ever be ready for that."

"Ready or not—it's time to go," Hailey said ushering Abby through the hotel room door.

The club was empty, just as predicted; except for a young woman, Abby did not know tending the bar. As she approached, she saw a sign hung behind the bar that read, "Loft for Lease." *She's moved or she's moving. That can't be good.*

"What can I get for you ladies?"

"Actually, I just read that sign about the loft?" she said more as a question than a statement.

"They won't be back until tomorrow, but since it's quiet in here, I can take you up to see it, if you're interested?"

*They. They who?* She wanted to know but didn't ask. "If you have time, we'd definitely like to see it." Maybe there would be some clues as to who "they" were up there. She suspected one of the *theys* would be Erin, but who was the other one.

"Follow me." As they climbed the stairs, Abby felt a rush of emotions as the memory of the last time she climbed those steps came flooding back to her. Once inside, the reality of the situation was starting to cause Abby to feel nauseous. The once empty space was now full of personal belongings. The previously bare walls were now very nicely decorated. There was a large eight by ten photograph of Erin and some other woman on the wall near the TV. She wanted to move closer to it, to get a better look, but was afraid that the bartender, who was now acting as their chaperone, might get suspicious. Instead, she headed for the kitchen and took notice of the two coffee cups in the sink, and the note on the fridge, which read, "I'll be home late tonight. Don't wait up. Love Meg."

"I think I've seen enough," she said to the bartender as she practically ran towards the door and down the stairs.

Hailey, not sure what to make of Abby's behaviour, tried to cover as best as she could; "I think she was hoping the kitchen would be bigger." She shrugged her shoulders at the woman who looked at her questioningly. "Thanks a lot for your time," she added as she walked quickly out the door to meet up with Abby who was already standing outside on the sidewalk.

"What happened in there?"

"She's clearly seeing someone. I don't know why I agreed to this."

"Come on let's go back to the hotel and have some dinner and a few drinks. You'll feel better."

The next night the two women stood once again on the sidewalk outside of ED's. "I can't believe you talked me into coming back here," Abby said resting her hand on the door handle unable to find the courage to pull it open.

"You have to see for yourself."

"Fine. Let's go."

The minute she walked in she spotted Erin working frantically behind the bar, joking with the customers and although she looked even better than Abby remembered, she clearly had changed. She knew she wasn't ready to face her yet and she was sure that either Erin didn't see her walk in or, even more disturbing, didn't remember her. She chose a table in a dark corner, which would allow her to observe without being seen.

She watched as a beautiful young woman made her way down the staircase, stopped at the bar, spoke to Erin, then gave her a hug and a kiss on the cheek before walking out the door. Abby felt her stomach tighten. She involuntarily clenched her fists and glared back over to the bar where Erin was now flirting with a beautiful blond woman who seemed to hang on her every word. Abby knew she had no right to feel the way she was feeling, but the rage was almost overpowering.

Hailey returned with their drinks completely oblivious to what Abby had witnessed. "Here, looks like you need these," she said as she placed two drinks in front of Abby who had already had several drinks before they left the hotel. "Care to tell me why you look like you want to kill someone?"

Abby did not reply she only motioned with her head for Hailey to look over at Erin with the woman at the bar.

"So. Maybe she's just being friendly." She was trying to remain optimistic, but even she, was having a hard time believing what she was saying. She was also beginning to regret bringing Abby back here, especially considering the amount of alcohol she had already consumed.

"What about the other one who just left?" Abby said referring to the young woman who had hugged and kissed Erin before leaving the club.

"I saw that, but she seemed so young I didn't really pay much attention to her." Hailey said hoping to find a way to settle Abby down quickly before she got out of hand.

"She came down from the loft," Abby said angrily.

She was clearly agitated, clearly drunk and Hailey feared she was soon going to do something stupid. "Maybe we should just go back to the hotel?" she suggested hoping Abby would agree, but knowing full well that she wouldn't.

"I'm not going anywhere."

Hailey begrudgingly took her seat next to Abby and watched as Erin and the voluptuous blonde made their way to the dance floor.

"Come on! We're dancing," Abby exclaimed as she roughly grabbed Hailey's arm and led her toward the dance floor.

Hailey knew Abby was thinking irrationally and that she was capable of anything in her current state. She also knew that trying to resist her would likely only cause a bigger scene so she followed along despite her apprehension. Abby held her much closer than necessary and cupped her ass firmly. She knew she had a choice to make and either one would undoubtedly result in some sort of spectacle. She could forcibly put a stop to Abby's little display or she could play along with it. Since she didn't know how Abby would react to a sudden, but gentle knee to the groin, she decided to play along.

Erin was startled at first to see Abby. One joyous moment after her brain registered who she was looking at it registered that she wasn't alone. She gracefully guided Joanne over to an area of the dance floor that put her in clear view of Abby. The second their eyes met for the first time there was an undeniable spark. A distant longing. An "I'm not done with you yet" look. Abby's body trembled at the recognition of desire in Erin's eyes. She pulled Hailey even closer and slid her hand between them to cup her breast.

"Two can play at that game," Erin mumbled to herself. "Do you mind playing along for a few minutes, Joanne?"

"What do you have in mind?"

"Just follow my lead," she said as she spun Joanne around so that she could meet Abby's eyes again. She gently pulled Joanne's head back and began kissing her neck causing her to whimper in appreciation all the while keeping hold of Abby's eyes.

Abby noted the challenge in Erin's gaze and followed suit capturing Hailey's neck with her lips for a moment before raising the stakes by shifting her position slightly so that her thigh was planted firmly between Hailey's legs. Abby watched Erin's eyes grow dark with arousal as they replicated each other's actions completely oblivious to their dance partners. *It feels like she's fucking me with her eyes. That's sooo hot!*

"Erin, honey!" Joanne said as she firmly gripped her arm. "This has to stop ... unless of course, you're planning on taking me upstairs when this song is over," she said as she struggled for breath.

"God, Joanne!" She took a step back so she could see Joanne's face. "I'm so sorry!" Erin said as a wave of shame rushed through her at the sight of Joanne's heavy breathing and heavily lidded eyes. "I didn't mean to get so carried away."

"I'm not really sure what you're trying to accomplish, but I know it has nothing to do with me." She stepped away and adjusted her clothes so that she looked presentable. "So I'm going to leave now." *Thank God, I got new batteries for my vibrator yesterday.* "A little fair warning." She chuckled softly. "Next time I'm not going to stop. I'll take what's mine. By force, if necessary!" She kissed Erin on the cheek and made her way out of the club.

Hailey reached for Abby's face and turned her head so that their eyes met.

Suddenly, realizing where she was and what she was doing, Abby started to apologize. "Hailey, I'm sor ..." The sting of Hailey's hand slapping her across the face silenced her. *I guess I deserved that.*

"Don't you ever do that to me again!" she said angrily. "I'm going back to the hotel. You're on your own." She stormed out, leaving Abby standing there in a daze.

*Son of a bitch!* She was drunk, feeling terrible about using Hailey and was still caught somewhere between a jealous rage and unbelievably aroused as she started to make her way to the restrooms at the other end of the club.

"WATCH WHERE YOU'RE GOING!" The woman shouted as Abby bumped into her roughly. "God, it's you!" she added when she turned to see who had bumped into her.

"Karen! What a pleasant surprise!" she said sarcastically as she met Karen's angry gaze. Abby was had a lot of pent up anger and who better to let it out on than someone who deserved it.

The already volatile situation was growing tenser by the minute. There was a crowd forming around the two women as they circled each other throwing insults back and forth. Abby had had way too much to drink and was an emotional mess. The sight of Karen was only fuelling her rage.

"Erin! We've got trouble!" Frankie said as she pointed to the crowd gathering around the two women.

"Who is it?" she asked trying to prepare herself. Since she knew most of the women, she knew how to diffuse most of these situations without much trouble.

"One of them is Karen, but I can't see the other."

"Fuck! Who let Karen in? She's barred for life," she asked as they pushed and shoved their way through the crowd.

Despite being drunk, Abby's reflexes were still quick enough to duck Karen's first punch. Her return punch managed to graze just the side of Karen's head as she moved out of the way. "I'll kill you!" she shouted as her second punch missed Abby again.

Erin stopped in her tracks when she saw that it was Abby who was fighting with Karen.

"It's Abby!"

"*The* Abby?" Frankie asked. She was surprised that Erin would ever find anyone who would behave this way attractive.

"Uh! Huh!" Part of her wanted to join in with the crowd and watch Abby give Karen a taste of her own medicine, but she knew how drunk she was and couldn't conscientiously let this continue. "You take Karen. I'll take Abby."

The two women continued to circle each other each of them waiting for the right opportunity to connect. "ABBY STOP!" Erin shouted over the sound of the crowd causing Abby to look up in her direction. Unfortunately, Frankie had not yet reached Karen and she let loose with a right hook that caught the unprepared Abby squarely in the jaw, sending her tumbling backwards into a table. She quickly got up, shook it off, and was charging back toward the grinning woman when Erin stepped in front of her and pushed her back. By then Frankie, with the help of a couple other women, had restrained Karen and were in the process of escorting her out the door.

"Let me go!" she said as she struggled to free herself from Erin's hold. She lost her balance during the struggle and ended up falling squarely into a chair.

Erin knew she would not be able to hold her back much longer so she sat in Abby's lap and wrapped her legs around the chair as leverage against the still struggling woman.

"Get off of me!" Abby shouted again trying in vain to push the woman off of her.

"Damn it, Abby, sit still!" Erin said sternly. "Where's your girlfriend?" She was hoping the other woman would be able to get Abby out of there.

"I don't have a girlfriend."

"Oh! I forgot you don't do girlfriends." Thankfully, Abby was calming down as the adrenaline was leaving her body. "Then, where's the woman you were trying to fuck on my dance floor?" she added sarcastically.

"She left," Abby replied calmly. She was starting to get sleepy and just wanted to lie down. "Went back to the hotel."

Frankie arrived with a bag of ice and Erin stood to assess Abby's condition. Her jaw was swollen and red, but she did not appear to have sustained any serious injuries. She handed the bag of ice to Abby who tried as best as possible to hold it to her face. Erin stopped Meg who had returned and filled her in on the details.

"Can you help me get her upstairs?"

"You can't be serious?" Meg replied.

"She'll pass out on the couch. It'll be fine." Erin hoped that was the case, but she wasn't sure what to expect from her. "She's nearly passed out as it is, there's no way we're going to get her back to the hotel like this."

"So, call the cops and let them handle it," Meg replied coolly. "I can't believe that *this* is your Abby," she added as she pointed to Abby who was slumped back in the chair barely able to hold her head up.

"Just shut up and help me."

# Chapter Seventeen

"Wake up!" Meg shouted, kicking at the sofa where Abby lay.

"Where am I?" Abby asked jolted awake. "Oh God!" she said, realizing suddenly she was on Erin's couch. "How did I get here?"

"Your friend left you here and Aunt Erin didn't think she could get you back to the hotel so she decided to let you sleep up here."

"Shh! Don't yell! Um … Did you say Aunt Erin?"

"Yes, why?"

"I thought that …"

"You thought we were a couple?" Meg said laughing out loud "You're an idiot!"

Abby nodded her agreement while holding her throbbing head in her hands.

"I didn't do anything stupid last night, did I?" Abby asked concerned that she had no recollection of the evening before.

"You mean something stupid like trying to kiss her and telling her you love her?" she smiled. "Oh, and starting a fight with Karen."

"I didn't!"

"You did."

"God, what have I done?" she said as she gently pressed on her jaw trying to determine how badly it hurt.

"Abby, why did you come here? You look like hell by the way"

"I feel like hell. Must you keep shouting? I'm not sure why I came here. I just wanted to see her again and apologize for walking out on her and then I saw the two of you together I freaked out. Then I saw her with that blonde and really got confused. Was she angry about last night?"

"I don't think so. She told me to be nice to you if you woke up before she got back."

"And this is you being nice to me?"

"I have no reason to be nice to you. I wish you hadn't come back here. She was finally getting on with her life and then you come back."

"What do you mean?"

"She said she couldn't stop thinking about you. I even set her up with Joanne, the blonde from last night … but she won't move on. I'm not sure if I believe in love at first sight, but if there ever was a case of it, she has it. I don't know what you did to her, but you wrecked her for anyone else."

"I didn't do anything to her." Abby thought back to the night she'd spent there. "But I think I know how she feels. I haven't really been able to stop thinking about her either," she said remembering how she'd tried to occupy her mind with things to block out the thought of Erin.

"Why did you wait so long to come back then?" Meg said accusingly.

"I don't know. Fear, I guess. I wanted to forget. I tried to forget. I wouldn't have come back at all if I hadn't had to come back again for work."

"She's going to be back soon; maybe you should get yourself together before she gets back. I've got some clothes you can borrow and a new toothbrush you can have."

"You don't have to do that you know. I could just go back to the hotel."

"Oh no you won't! You're not running away this time. You *will* be here when she gets home, even if I have to tie you to a chair."

Abby laughed at what Erin would think if she walked in and saw her tied to a chair.

"Where did she go anyway?"

"She had to meet some friends for brunch this morning," Meg said matter-of-factly

Meg handed Abby a bottle of aspirin and some clothes and motioned for her to go get ready. Abby was suddenly very nervous. Was she ready to face the possibility that what she'd really felt for Erin was love and more frightening than that, what if Erin had moved on despite Meg's notion to the contrary. She could still run, but her mother's words came back to her with conviction. "Follow your heart Abigail, nothing else matters."

Meg's clothes fit her well although the jeans were a little long. Meg was beautiful; taller than Erin, but she had the same natural beauty about her and the same confident stride. She should have realized their similarities last night, but she couldn't see past her own insecurities.

Abby took a long shower and joined Meg, who was reading a magazine, at the table.

"You look better!" Meg said glancing at Abby.

"I feel better," Abby said. "Thanks for the clothes."

"You're actually kind of cute, you know? And you have very pretty eyes. Aunt Erin seems to have a thing for blue eyes."

"Cute? Thanks, I guess. But cute is not the word I'd use to describe myself," Abby replied self-consciously at Meg's assessment.

"That's just my opinion; Aunt Erin said she found you alluring and sexy."

"We really shouldn't be talking about this anymore," Abby said feeling awkward talking to Erin's niece about these things. "Why don't we talk about something else?"

They talked for a few minutes about Meg's classes and Abby started to relax, finally. Her headache was nearly gone when the door opened. Erin stopped mid-step when she caught sight of Abby sitting at the table. Abby looked up and instantly captured Erin's eyes. Neither of them said a word. They allowed their eyes to speak for them. Abby's eyes were apologetic and Erin's were soft and forgiving.

Meg, suddenly feeling very much in the way, got up and said she'd see them later even though she was sure neither of them heard her.

They remained silent for several minutes looking into each other's eyes for answers to questions they didn't know they even had. Erin broke away first. "Hi!" she said, not sure what else to say that very moment.

"Hi!" Abby replied nervously.

"How do you feel? How's your jaw."

"My jaw's fine, but I'm much better now that you're home," she said pathetically.

"Oh! Poor thing. Was little Meg mean to you?" Erin teased.

"Yeah, she even told me I was cute. Do you think I'm cute?"

"No. Definitely not cute. Charming, elusive and sexy, yes. But not cute," Erin replied blushing slightly.

"I'm sorry I left."

"Don't be sorry, Abby. You weren't ready to give me what I needed and I wasn't ready for what I really wanted. I should have never tried to seduce you."

"Should I not have come back here?" she questioned hesitantly.

"Depends on why you're back."

"I can't stop thinking about you; I've tried. Oh have I tried."

"Really?"

"Really."

A single tear fell to Erin's cheek and Abby immediately went to her, wrapping her arms around her waist pulling her close.

"Erin?"

"Yes."

"Kiss me."

"I thought you'd never ask," Erin replied. She smiled and looked deeply into Abby's eyes for the truth before taking her lips with her own so passionately it ignited sparks of something that Erin didn't even know existed within her. Abby instantly remembered their first kiss; it had been just as powerful and she hadn't been kissed that way since.

"So, where do we go from here?" Abby said pulling away first needing a break to allow the blood to return to her brain.

"I don't know. I didn't expect you to come back." She sighed and fought hard to contain a yawn.

"You look tired. Let's go take a nap," Abby suggested.

"I didn't get much sleep. I kept getting up to check on you."

"Thank you." She was moved by the thought of Erin checking on her while she was passed out on the couch. "Come on," Abby said before wrapping her arm around Erin's waist and leading her to the bedroom.

"Are you sure?" Erin asked putting her hand over Abby's, entwining their fingers.

"Yes, I'm very sure, and this time when you wake up, I'll still be here," she said kissing her softly on the cheek. "I promise."

Erin drifted off to sleep quickly in her arms. With their bodies still fully clothed, Abby couldn't help but remember their first night together. This felt the same, but was entirely different because she knew she wouldn't run away this time. "Erin?" Abby whispered and waited to make sure Erin was asleep before continuing. "I think I'm falling in love with you."

They slept peacefully until Erin woke to the sound of Meg rummaging around "Abby?" Erin called waking her gently; "I've got to get ready for work."

"Okay, I should go back to the hotel to check on my friend anyhow," Abby replied.

"Will you stay with me tonight?" Erin asked

"I'd love to stay if you want me to."

"I definitely want you to," Erin answered, kissing Abby softly on the lips as she walked her to the door.

"Okay, I'll be back in a few hours."

"Abby?" Erin called as Abby reached the bottom of the staircase.

"Yeah!"

"I think I'm falling in love with you too."

Abby was certain her feet did not touch a single step on the way back up the stairs, taking Erin in her arms and kissing her as if her survival depended solely on that one kiss. "I thought you were sleeping?" she said as she begrudgingly withdrew from the kiss.

"I thought I was dreaming," Erin replied, relieved that she had not dreamt hearing those words.

"I'll be back as soon as I can," Abby said floating down the stairs.

Erin stood for a few moments stabilizing herself against the wall, her knees weakened by the kiss. "I'm in so much trouble," she said to herself, amazed at the way she felt when Abby kissed her.

"Hailey!" Abby called out as she entered the hotel room.

"Abs! Are you okay? I was beginning to worry." She was very angry with Abby about what happened the night before, but she started to get concerned when Abby didn't come back to the room by mid afternoon.

"I thought you'd still be pissed at me."

"I am, but we'll have that discussion later. Where have you been?"

"I'm sorry!" she said dreamily. "I should have called, but things happened so fast, I didn't have a chance."

"What happened?"

"Turns out the young girl is Meg; Erin's niece."

"God, Abs, you're such an idiot sometimes."

"I know. But it's okay now. Very well, as a matter of fact," Abby said gathering her toiletries and heading for the bathroom.

"Tell me what happened ... who was the blonde? Whose clothes are you wearing?" Hailey asked impatiently as she followed her into the bathroom.

Abby undressed and hopped in the shower continuing her conversation with Hailey. "The blonde is some woman Meg tried to set her up with, but I guess they're just friends. These are Meg's clothes; she lent them to me after reading me the riot act while Erin was gone out."

"That bad!"

"Well it wouldn't have been that bad if I hadn't had such a hangover. She's actually really cool."

"Then what happened?" she said handing Abby a towel when she stepped out of the shower.

"Then, she came home, forgave me for my stupidity and I told her I was falling in love with her."

"Abigail Grant, in love! Well, I never thought the day would come."

"Neither did I friend, neither did I," she replied as she looked at herself in the mirror and gently brushed her fingers over her bruised jaw. "I'm so sorry about last night, Hailey. I didn't mean for it to get so out of hand. What are you going to tell Toni?"

"I didn't do that to your face did I?" Hailey asked seeing the bruise on Abby's jaw for the first time.

"Oh! I forgot to tell you, I got in a fight with Lauren's ex right after you left last night."

"The psycho one?"

"That's the one. I don't remember much about last night, though. I remember you slapping me and then the next thing I remember is waking up on Erin's couch."

"I'm sorry I slapped you, but I was pissed. It shouldn't have happened, but I didn't stop you, so it was partly my fault. I still can't believe you did that, or that I let you."

"I truly am sorry. I feel terrible about it." For once in her life, she really did feel badly about what she'd done. Hailey wasn't her little play thing any more and what she had done was wrong on so many levels. She took advantage of their friendship and their past.

"I don't think we should tell Toni," Hailey said. "It wasn't like it meant anything to either of us. It just happened and it won't happen again. What would be the point in telling her?"

"Are you sure? I know you love her and if you want to tell her, I'll take full responsibility." She didn't want her to feel like she had to keep it a secret for her sake. It would probably be best not to tell her since it didn't mean anything, but she wanted Hailey to do what she thought was best.

"I just don't see the point in telling her. She knows what our relationship was like. Can we just forget about it?"

"If that's what you want. Let me know if you change your mind. You want to go grab some dinner?"

"Sure, but wouldn't you rather be with Erin?"

"Well yes, not that I don't enjoy your company, but she's working tonight and I don't think I can stand to sit there for the whole night knowing I have to wait until her shift is over before I can have my way with her."

"I see, so I'm a distraction. Haven't you slept with her yet?"

"Not yet. Actually, on the way over here I started to think about what you said to me when you met Toni. You know, about waiting until you got to know her."

"Are you sure you don't have a concussion or something?" Hailey asked.

"I don't know. Maybe I do. I just need to make some changes and this would be a good start. It won't be easy, when all I want to do is rip her clothes off; but I want to do this right. I really want this to work."

"Who are you, and what have you done with Abby?" Hailey joked and pulled her into a friendly embrace. "I'm proud of you."

"Don't go singing my praises just yet; I don't know how much willpower I have."

"You'll be fine. You've finally got your priorities in order," Hailey said encouragingly as they left their hotel room.

"Meg, who's your favourite aunt?" Erin joked.

"What do you want, Aunt Erin?" Meg replied accusingly.

"Do you think you could maybe find some place else to stay tonight. Just for tonight, I promise. Please?"

"I'm way ahead of you. When I saw Tom this afternoon I asked him if he would mind if I spent the night. The only reason I'm here is to get a few things, then I'm gone."

"You're the best, kiddo!"

"I know!" Meg replied jokingly.

Hailey and Abby enjoyed a nice dinner at the hotel restaurant then Hailey went back to the room to wait for Toni to arrive. Hailey had felt it a bit of a waste for Toni to fly in for just two nights, but it was all her schedule would allow, and now that Abby had hooked up with Erin, she was very glad Toni would be there to keep her company.

## Chapter Eighteen

When Abby finally made it to the club, it was well after nine and the place was packed. She quickly made her way through the sea of women and found an empty seat at the bar. Erin was busy, but she could not contain the smile that appeared on her lips at the sight of Abby. For a few moments, before Abby arrived, Erin was starting to worry that maybe she wouldn't come back. Her heart wanted to believe that she would, but her mind would not allow it.

When she finally got a moment to catch her breath she brought a drink over to Abby and set it in front of her. "Here you go, darling," Erin said, capturing her eyes wondering what Abby was thinking. She looked scared. *Please don't run away again, Abby.* She wished she didn't have to work tonight so she could help Abby sort through what she was feeling.

Her thoughts were interrupted by Frankie's voice, "Erin, are you going to introduce me to your new friend?"

"Sorry, Frankie. Abby, this is my best friend, Frankie. Frankie this is my," there was a silent pause as Erin tried to come up with the best word to use to describe her relationship with Abby without scaring her off. "Um … this is Abby," she said awkwardly.

"Frankie, it's a pleasure to meet you," Abby said, extending her hand to the beautiful woman, surprised at the scrutinizing gaze she received in return.

"Likewise," she said before walking away.

Abby sat for several minutes pondering the thought that Erin had probably filled Frankie in on everything and that it was a natural reaction for her to want to protect her friend from the likes of someone like Abby.

"Abby, would you dance with me please?" Frankie said making her way from around the bar in a fashion that suggested there was no way for Abby to decline the invitation.

"Here we go," Abby whispered to herself, letting Frankie lead her to the dance floor.

There was a simultaneous "Aww!" throughout the crowd as Frankie took Abby into her arms. Frankie had always declined the women's invitations to dance, so they were suddenly very interested in whom it was that Frankie was dancing with.

"Abby!" Frankie said coldly. "If you do anything to hurt Erin, I will have to kill you."

Abby was certain, for some reason, that Frankie would be capable of such vengeance, but she blocked that thought out trying to find a way to gain the acceptance she so desperately needed this moment. Frankie's opinion could weigh heavily on their relationship especially since it was in such a fragile state.

"Listen, Frankie," Abby said looking her square in the eyes. "I know I've been a fool. I've made some terrible mistakes so far where Erin has been concerned, but I promise, from today forward, it will be my sole purpose in life to make her happy. I'll do whatever it takes to make it up to her." She was suddenly interrupted by a hand on her shoulder.

"May I cut in?" Erin said pushing Frankie away and gathering the panic stricken Abby into her arms.

"Hey," Abby said relieved to be away from Frankie's scrutiny for a few moments.

"Hey yourself, gorgeous," Erin said smiling, seeing the look of uncertainty in Abby's eyes. "Sorry about Frankie. What did she say to you?"

"Nothing I didn't deserve," Abby replied truthfully. "I've been such a fool, Erin. I shouldn't have waited so long to come back, and I shouldn't have left in the first place, and last night ..."

"Shh!" Erin said placing her finger on Abby's lips to silence her. "You're here now and that's all that matters." They danced in silence for a few minutes enjoying the comfort they were giving each other. Their bodies talking for them, letting each other know that everything would be okay. Erin's conveying an unconditional forgiveness, while Abby's conveyed a sense of security that she would not run away again.

"You mystify me," Abby said, nuzzling into Erin's neck as they danced.

"You fascinate me," Erin replied, pulling Abby closer, wanting to climb inside her.

Abby was amazed at the energy their bodies created together and she suddenly had to fight the urge to drag Erin back upstairs to show her exactly how she felt about her, despite her vow to wait. "Erin?"

"Yes, darling," she whispered into Abby's ear.

"Do you have to stay until closing?"

"Yes. Why?"

"No reason," Abby said. She pulled away a little trying to lessen the desire that was building within her at the feel of Erin's body so close to hers.

"Life is good," she mumbled to herself as she headed back to the bar to take her seat when the song ended. She watched Erin work, unable to avert her eyes for more than a second at a time. It was going to be a long night waiting for 2:00 AM to arrive especially when Erin kept looking back at her with a seductive smile. *God, does she even understand what she's doing to me right now?* Abby thought to herself, her body on fire.

Erin returned with a glass of water. "No more alcohol for you tonight," she said while putting the glass down in front of Abby who looked back at her questioningly. "I'd like you to be very aware of what I do to you later on." She finished with a smile that set Abby's insides into a frenzy.

This is going to be harder than I thought, Abby said to herself. Abby hadn't had a chance to tell Erin about her decision to wait a while and Erin was clearly planning on something happening tonight. She wondered how the woman, who clearly had other ideas, would receive her decision.

The subtle, but seductive glares, the gentle, but lingering touches—nothing had gone unnoticed between them and near the end of the night Abby was not sure she could take any more. Her resolve was fading quickly. She was no longer sure she could wait.

Hours later, as Abby stood gazing out the large picture window overlooking the city lights; Erin stepped up behind her and wrapped her arms around her waist. Abby sighed peacefully, treasuring this special moment as she folded her arms over Erin's. It was as if they were some place else; just the two of them; looking down at the world going about its business while they existed on some different plane in a different reality.

"Mmm, you smell good," Erin said as she nuzzled into Abby's neck torn between wanting to take her to bed and just stay where they were enjoying the simple pleasure of the moment.

Abby turned to face Erin, resting her hands casually on her shoulders and searched her eyes for understanding, for something to calm her fears. She was scared of what she was feeling. She had never felt like this before. She suddenly felt like she needed Erin. Her entire existence now seemed to revolve around Erin being a part of her life and she didn't want to screw it up.

Erin noticed Abby's hesitation, looked deeply into her fearful eyes and said, "I'm scared too." She was terrified to say the least. She knew what she was feeling was love and the thought that Abby might get scared and run away again terrified her. Now that she was back, Erin was not prepared to let her go again. She leaned down to capture Abby's lips with hers. Softly, tenderly, kissing away the fear.

When Erin made a move to guide them to the bedroom, Abby stood her ground and stopped her. "Erin?"

"What's wrong?"

"This is going to sound really lame, especially coming from me, but could we … I mean, would you mind if we …" she struggled to find the right words. "Can we wait a while?"

Erin was both surprised and relieved. She didn't expect this from Abby, but the fact that Abby wanted to wait meant that she was taking this possible relationship seriously and that she wasn't just another notch on Abby's belt.

"We can wait as long as you want," Erin replied and pulled Abby into her arms and kissed her softly on the lips.

"Do that again," Abby urged.

"You're not going to make this easy, are you?" Erin joked and kissed Abby again. "Come on. Let's try to get some sleep."

Abby was surprised at how easily she was able to fall asleep, despite the fact that Erin was resting comfortably in her arms. She had never had a more restful sleep in her entire life.

In the morning, Abby snuck out of bed and was in the kitchen cooking breakfast when Meg walked in.

"Hungry?" Abby asked.

"Not really," Meg said dejectedly.

"What's wrong?"

"My boyfriend is a jackass. He was talking in his sleep and kept mentioning his ex-girlfriend's name."

"Did you ask him about it? Maybe something triggered a memory or something. It may not have been that he was actually dreaming about her."

"He was clearly dreaming about her. I'll spare you the details, but there was no question about it."

"Sorry kiddo."

"Hello ladies!" Erin said cheerfully as she entered the room and kissed them each on the cheek. Meg quickly left the room, went to her bedroom and shut the door.

"Was it something I said?" Erin asked, astonished at Meg's sudden departure.

"No, but when you're done your breakfast you might want to go in there and talk to her though. She had a bad night," Abby suggested, wrapping her arms around Erin and inhaling the scent of her soap and shampoo. "God, you smell good!"

She quickly ushered Erin over to the table and set a plate of food down in front of her before she gave in to the ever-present temptation to take her to bed. She realized that she could easily get used to waking up with Erin and making her breakfast every day. Then she realized that she was going home tomorrow. Just the thought of leaving filled her with sadness. She had finally found the most amazing woman, who made her feel things she had never felt before, feelings she never thought she would feel and in twenty-four hours, she would be leaving again.

"What's wrong?" Erin asked, suddenly concerned at the look of sorrow on Abby's face.

She didn't want to spoil their day with the news, but she knew she had to tell her eventually. She reached for Erin's hand and held it in hers for several seconds before speaking. "I have to go home tomorrow."

"Oh!" Erin replied, shocked at the news. She knew Abby wouldn't be staying long, but she hadn't considered the possibility that she would be leaving tomorrow. There was so much she wanted to talk to her about, so many things she had yet to explore and learn about Abby. If she left tomorrow, would she come back?

"I was hoping we might have had more time together."

"I'm sorry. I didn't expect any of this." Abby was trembling, tears threatening. She had never experienced this imminent sense of loss before. "It all feels so overwhelming."

With that, Erin stood and pulled Abby up into her arms and embraced her. "I know, darling, I know." She, herself, was somewhat overwhelmed with her own feelings. Everything between them was so easy and felt so natural and so right. It was frightening that something so powerful could develop so quickly between two people and she couldn't shake the thought that Abby might bolt at any moment.

Erin sat back down, pulled Abby into her lap and changed the subject. "What would you like to do today?"

"I'm leaving that up to you, except that I would like you to meet my friends at some point," Abby replied.

"Is one of those friends, the one you were here with the other night?" Erin asked in a non-accusatory tone.

Abby blushed and took Erin's hand in hers. "I'm sorry about that. I was so upset that you were with someone that I wanted to show you what you were missing. And yes, one of them is her."

"I was just as responsible for what happened that night as you were. And Joanne, the woman I was dancing with, will probably never speak to me again."

Abby proceeded to tell Erin everything there was to tell about her unusual relationship with Hailey and finished by telling her that if it wasn't for Hailey's encouragement, she probably wouldn't have returned.

"I'll have to remember to thank her. I don't know what I would have done if you never came back." She kissed her on the cheek.

"Why don't you see if they're free for lunch? Then afterwards, we can go for a walk. There's something I want to show you."

"Okay. I'll call them, and get ready. In the mean time, you better go talk to Meg," Abby replied.

While showering, Abby started to regret her suggestion that the four of them go for lunch. She feared that Hailey and Erin might not get along. Since Abby, Hailey and Toni were about the same age and were all in relatively the same field of work, she was concerned that Erin might not fit in. She was also worried that Erin might harbour some resentment toward Hailey because of their little display on the dance floor a few nights earlier.

Abby's apprehension over their lunch plans was short-lived. She had worried for nothing. The four of them got along remarkably well. By the end of lunch, they were talking like long lost friends.

After their lunch, they said their goodbyes and headed their separate ways. Erin pulled Abby closer to her in a protective manner as they walked through some ominous looking alleys she used as short cuts to arrive at her final destination.

"Where are we?" Abby asked as they stood in front of an old abandoned warehouse.

"You'll see," Erin replied before unlocking the door and flipping the lights on.

"Wow!" Abby said once her eyes adjusted to the light. A lot of the work had been completed on the new club and even Erin had been impressed with the outcome. "What is this place?"

"Follow me," Erin replied and headed directly toward the back of the building and opened another door that led to a hallway. She produced another key and unlocked another door. "Watch your step," she said as she made her way through the maze of boxes and building materials, which were scattered, across the floor.

Abby stood dumfounded for several minutes taking in the amazing sight. Although incomplete and totally unfurnished, Abby could tell that this was Erin's new home. Every detail screamed of her quiet strength and passionate freedom. They were standing in the living room and from there; Abby could see the amazing open kitchen, with its dark cherry custom cabinets, slate countertops and stainless steel built-it appliances.

Abby was imagining herself in that kitchen preparing a meal for Erin when Erin took her by the hand and led her down a short hallway to her expansive bedroom. The slate floor which covered the rest of the apartment stopped at the bedroom door and gave way to the rustic charms of old wood floorboards. The walls were painted in rich colours which reminded her of the leaves changing back home.

Erin walked over to Abby and wrapped loving arms around her waist. "So, what do you think?"

"It's so …" Abby searched her vocabulary for the right word to describe how she felt about what she was seeing. Nothing seemed to convey her exact reaction. "It's so you," she replied and kissed Erin softly on the lips.

"Does that mean you like it?"

"It means; I lo … Like it a lot." She corrected herself quickly. Had she really almost said she loved it, therefore meaning she loved Erin? She stepped back slightly from Erin's embrace wanting to see the expression on her face. Hopefully she hadn't noticed the slip up.

Erin was unable to contain the smile that formed on her lips. Abby had almost said the words she longed to hear. She new she had to ease out of this situation carefully because she could see how uncomfortable Abby was. "Good, because I think it likes you a lot too."

# Chapter Nineteen

After leaving the new club, Erin took Abby for long romantic ride along the coast, where they stopped for a quick dinner before heading back home.

The remainder of their last evening together was spent cuddling on the couch watching movies. Abby could not believe how much she was enjoying this simple but intimate evening. She had never done anything like this before and never had she felt so close to anyone before. Despite the fact that the ongoing kissing and gentle caressing were fuelling her burning desire to make love to Erin, she knew that these few intimate hours would be more meaningful than what would undoubtedly be the best sex of her life.

"Abby?" Erin said breathlessly.

"Yes?" she replied and rested her head on Erin's shoulder.

"Have you changed your mind about waiting?"

"No. Is that a problem?"

"No, but it will be, if you don't stop touching me there," she said before taking Abby's wandering hand in hers.

"Sorry. Do you think this is stupid?"

"Not at all, but it might help if you explain to me why you made that decision."

"I have no doubt that we'll be compatible in bed, but I do have some doubts about the rest of it, and I want to be sure about some of those things before we do something that might jeopardize a great friendship if things don't work out between us."

"You've put a lot of thought into this. To be completely honest, I was surprised when you said you wanted to wait. But it was a nice surprise." She kissed Abby tenderly before continuing. "Am I to assume that we'll be seeing each other again then?" she asked hesitantly, trying to gauge Abby's commitment to their relationship without sounding needy or scaring her away.

"As often as possible," Abby replied evenly, completely unaware of Erin's growing insecurity.

"Will you be seeing other people when you go back home?" She knew the question was inappropriate, but it had to be asked.

Abby found the question offensive, but she understood why Erin felt it necessary to ask. She thought she would have proved her intentions toward this relationship by now, but apparently, it would take more time.

"No. I won't be seeing other people. I don't want to see other people."

"Good, because I don't want you to see anyone but me."

Abby woke to the bright sunlight creeping through the blinds into her eyes. Neither woman had moved the entire night. *God this feels so right.* She glanced over at the clock and realized with great sadness that it was nearly time to go. She tried to untangle herself from Erin's body without waking her, but the second she moved Erin grabbed her arm and whispered, "Stay."

"I can't. I have to get ready. My flight leaves in two hours." She pulled away and nearly ran into the bathroom to hide the tears she knew where coming.

"I meant, stay forever," Erin said knowing Abby couldn't hear her. What was she thinking? As wonderful as their weekend had been, they really did not know each other at all. How could she feel so strongly about wanting to be with Abby forever? It was too soon for any of this.

"I'm going to miss you so much," Abby said as she snuggled into Erin's neck while they said their goodbyes. *I don't know that I'll be able to breathe without you.* These feelings were so foreign to Abby she wasn't at all sure she would make it through the week.

"I know. It'll be okay." She hoped it would. What if Abby freaked out and decided to run again? What if Abby didn't share her feelings? Her emotions were scattered, she was feeling too many things right now to think clearly. She kissed Abby one last time before walking her out to the waiting cab. She gave Hailey and Toni a friendly wave and watched as Abby once again left with a piece of her heart.

It was at some point thirty thousand feet over Wyoming that reality set in. Who was she kidding? She glanced over at Hailey and Toni. They were holding hands, talking and giggling. Abby had no idea how to be a part of a couple. She couldn't be someone's girlfriend. She had no idea what that even meant. She could never make Erin happy. The feelings she felt for Erin were so strong that it had been painful to leave her. She couldn't fathom how much it would hurt when Erin finally realized that Abby wasn't who she wanted. She had no choice. She had to end this before she got in any deeper.

By the time the plane landed, she had a plan. It wasn't a great plan, but it was a plan nonetheless. She would simply disappear for a while. Erin wouldn't be able to find her to tell her that the weekend had been a mistake. She would not even tell Hailey where she was going.

She drove blindly toward the cabin, not even bothering to stop by her house. She was so distraught she didn't care that the electricity and water had been shut off for the winter. She lit a fire in the fireplace and immediately got to work on the first of three cases of beer she found stored in the pantry.

After ignoring the first three calls from Erin, she finally shut her cell phone off. Her only objective was to forget Erin.

It had been three days and Erin still had not been able to reach Abby. She had left several messages for her and received no response. Initially she had been concerned, thinking maybe something had happened to Abby, but as time went on, she was painfully aware that Abby had run away again. She wasn't just another of Abby's flings and she knew it. She felt it. They shared a special connection, a powerful bond. If she let Abby run away this time, she knew she'd be doing them both an injustice.

"Frankie, can you work the rest of the week for me?" Erin asked while wiping down the bar.

"Sure. Why?"

"I'm going to Michigan."

"Why are you wasting your time on her?" Frankie said with a hint of disdain in her voice.

"Because I love her, and I know she loves me. She's just scared." Erin hoped. She didn't want to consider the possibility that Abby didn't feel what she felt.

"I'm looking for Abigail Grant," Erin said nervously to the older woman sitting behind the desk, answering the phones.

"Oh! No! She's not in. Was she expecting you? I don't have anything scheduled for her today," Ruth replied frantically.

Erin thought the woman seemed flustered. At least she had the right place. There was only one CG Designs in the phone book and she hoped that this was it.

"No, she wasn't expecting me. Do you know when she might be in?"

"I honestly don't know. She left me a voice mail first thing Monday, before I even got to work, telling me to reschedule all of her appointments."

"You haven't heard from her then?"

"No. Not a peep! It's very unlike her not to check in, especially since Carson isn't back to work yet."

"Would Hailey be in?"

"She's been swamped with all of Abby's work, but I'll try." Erin stood as patiently as possible as Ruth dialled Hailey's extension. "Can I ask your name?"

"Erin Davis," she replied in an even tone.

"Hailey will be right up. Would you like a coffee or something while you wait?"

"No thank you."

Erin spotted Hailey walking down the hall and met her halfway. "Where is she?"

"She's not with you?" Hailey asked.

"No. I haven't seen her since she left with you and she isn't returning any of my calls." Erin sounded frantic. She hadn't slept much in the last three days and she was an emotional mess.

"She kind of freaked out on the plane," Hailey recalled suddenly. "I mean, she was fine, happier than I've ever seen her, and then all of a sudden, she just got all weird and quiet. I asked what was wrong, but you know how she is?"

"When she didn't show up for work on Monday, I just figured she went back to L.A."

"So you haven't heard from her at all either?" Erin's anger and hurt now verging on concern. Maybe something happened to her.

"Not a word. I know she's not at her house because I stopped by yesterday and it didn't look like anyone had been there for days."

"Where would she go?"

"I don't know," Hailey replied, suddenly sharing some of Erin's concern. "Let me call her mom."

Erin sat impatiently drumming her finger against her knee while Hailey dialled Helena Morris's number.

"Hi, Mrs. Morris. It's Hailey."

"Good morning, Hailey. How are you?"

"I'm fine Mrs. Morris. Have you heard from Abby lately?"

Erin looked at her expectantly, hoping that Mrs. Morris had heard from Abby.

"No dear, I haven't. Is something wrong?" Hailey shook her head from side to side to let Erin know what Mrs. Morris's response had been.

"No. Nothing's wrong. I just can't seem to find her. Is there somewhere she would go if she was upset?"

"Well, if she's not with you, then I really don't know ... Unless she went to the cabin. It would be really cold up there if she did. Bill and I closed it up a few weeks ago and turned off the water and electricity. Are you sure she's okay?"

"I'm sure she's fine. Could you give me the directions to the cabin, so I can go see if she's there?"

Erin watched intently as Hailey jotted down the directions Mrs. Morris was rattling off.

"Thanks, Mrs. Morris. I'll give you a call when I find her." Hailey hung up the phone and contemplated her options.

She could drive Erin to the cabin and pass up the nice quiet evening she had planned with Toni or she could let Erin make the trip on her own, not knowing what she'd find when she got there. Hailey wasn't sure why Abby had disappeared, so she had no idea what her condition would be. She could even be with another woman; definitely not something Erin needed to see right now.

She genuinely liked Erin, and thought she was good for Abby. The fact that she came all the way to Michigan to find her meant something. She had no idea why Abby was acting the way she was, but she was going to do whatever she could to help. Hailey quickly left a message for Toni, explaining the situation and apologizing for disrupting their plans for the evening. Twenty minutes later, they were headed toward the cabin.

When they pulled into the driveway, Hailey immediately saw Abby's car. "She's here," she said, only slightly relieved. She still had no idea what she was going to find inside.

"Stay here for a few minutes. Let me go in first," she ordered. She wanted to get an idea of what Abby's state of mind was before letting Erin talk to her.

Hailey found her sitting in the great room staring at the still glowing embers from a long ago extinguished fire. Beer cans littered the floor and the couch around her. She was still dressed in the same clothes she had worn on the flight home three days before.

If Abby was shocked or startled by Hailey's presence, she didn't show it. She appeared almost catatonic, not even moving when Hailey knelt down in front of her.

"Abs? Are you okay?"

"What have I done?" Abby said despondently.

"I don't know, Abby. What *have* you done?"

"I had what I wanted and I just threw it all away."

"Threw what away?"

"I hurt her. I did it on purpose."

"I don't understand."

"I ran again. I just shut her out."

"And you regret doing this?"

"It's the biggest mistake I've ever made. She must hate me."

"When are you going to learn that you can run from people, places or things, but you can't run away from your feelings?"

"I want to go home."

"There's someone here who wants to talk to you first," Hailey said gently, motioning for Erin, who was now standing at the doorway, to come in.

"Thank-you," Erin said to Hailey as she approached the two women.

Hailey smiled sympathetically, stood up and whispered, "She'll be okay. She's just scared." She called Toni to let her know she was on her way home and drove away, confident that things would be fine.

"Hi," Erin said softly.

Abby recognized the voice but wouldn't meet her eyes. She couldn't believe Erin had come all this way to find her. She was ashamed of what she had done and embarrassed that Erin was witnessing her in her in what could only be described as her weakest moment.

"What do you want from me?" Abby asked evenly, despite the fact that her emotions were all over the map.

"Right now, all that I want is, for you to let me take you home," Erin replied softly.

Abby finally found the courage to look at her. She never expected Erin to come looking for her. Abby thought Erin looked sad. She knew it was her fault. She stood slowly and Erin draped a jacket around her before walking her out to the car.

The two-hour long drive back to Abby's house was made in silence. Erin was relieved that Abby was okay, but the relief was short lived, as anger and hurt began to take shape once again. She was anxious to get the eminent discussion over with, but Abby was in no condition to talk just yet. She hadn't showered in days and apparently had consumed nothing but beer during her three-day hiatus.

She riffled through Abby's kitchen cupboards, desperate to find anything that could be concocted into something resembling a meal. She had nearly given up and ordered a pizza when she found some tomatoes and peppers in the fridge. A few minutes later, her famous spaghetti sauce was simmering on the stove.

Abby stood sheepishly outside the kitchen door, dressed in an old pair of Michigan State sweats. She willed her feet to move forward, but they wouldn't.

The sight of Erin, standing in her kitchen making dinner, caused her breath to catch. How could she still be there after the way Abby had hurt her? She didn't know what to say or do to make things right again.

"Sit down, Abby," Erin said gently. She couldn't believe how vulnerable Abby looked standing there. She looked so innocent and fragile. She had seen Abby at her best and at her worst, but this vulnerable side was extremely adorable and unexpected.

Abby slowly made her way to the table and silently sat down. Erin placed a plate of pasta in front of her and sat down across from her. They ate in silence. Abby couldn't find the words to convey what she wanted to say. She felt like a prisoner of her own mind.

Erin watched in awe as Abby looked at her, opened her mouth and closed it again without saying a word. She did this repeatedly. Under different circumstances, it would have been comical.

Mercifully, she said something. It wasn't what Erin expected to hear, but it was a start.

"Why did you come after me?"

"Because, I love you."

"But I hurt you."

"Yes. And I'm angry with you, but it doesn't mean I suddenly stopped loving you."

Abby sat for a moment, trying to wrap her head around the fact that Erin wasn't going anywhere. "What if I can't be who you need me to be?"

"Don't you understand, that I don't want you to be anyone but who you are? I don't understand how or why, but I fell in love with you the moment I met you."

Abby was astonished and relieved. She didn't know what Erin expected of her and she didn't think she'd be able to change.

"I don't know how to do this."

"Just love me, Abby. And don't ever leave me again." She stood up, pulled Abby into her arms, and held her.

"I'm sorry. I just … I was so scared. I didn't know what else to do."

"Next time, just talk to me. We can work through it together."

"Erin?"

"Hum?"

"Kiss me."

Erin smiled and pulled Abby closer. "I thought you'd never ask?"

After a long, sweet kiss, Abby pulled away. "So, does this mean we're okay now?" she asked, having never been in this situation before.

"Very okay," she said as she reached for a bottle of wine and led Abby to the living room. She put several oversized pillows down in front of the fireplace and they cuddled into each other enjoying the beauty of the moment. The house was very romantic; Abby thought it odd that she had never noticed it before. The vaulted ceilings accented by the wooden beams added to the charm of the natural stone fireplace. It was very cozy suddenly. It had always felt empty, but not anymore.

She finally understood what her mother meant when she said, "You'll know it when it happens." Abby was in love. Letting go of her insecurities and fears was liberating. It was intoxicating.

Abby was freezing when she woke to the sound of Erin calling her name. The physical and emotional stress of the day had caught up with both of them and the cold chill that remained when the fire went out snapped them back to reality.

"Sorry, I guess we fell asleep. Do you want to go upstairs to bed?"

Erin nodded and Abby pulled her to her feet, kissed her soundly and led her upstairs. Erin stopped dead in her tracks in front of the large picture window in Abby's bedroom. "This is beautiful Abby," she said as she admired the view of the steep, moonlit, rolling hill that led to a fast flowing creek below.

"Yeah it is. In the summer, you can't see the creek for the leaves on the trees. But this time of year is my favourite. When the leaves change color and give way, one by one, to the view of the creek, it's amazing. I'm glad you like it; I've never had anyone up here before. It's kind of nice to see it for the first time again through your eyes." Abby stepped in front of Erin and pulled her arms around her from behind. As they stood there silently, gazing out at the beautiful landscape, Abby remembered how her father had told her she overpaid for this piece of property. At this very moment she was certain it was priceless.

"Thank you for sharing it with me," Erin said turning Abby to face her.

"Thank you, for making me want to share it," Abby replied, gently caressing Erin's beautiful face. "Let's go to bed."

# Chapter Twenty

The next several weeks were an exercise in discipline and creative travel. Abby would fly to L.A. on Friday evenings to spend the weekend with Erin since she couldn't leave the bar. Erin would then fly back to Lansing with her Monday mornings, so that Abby could go to work, only to fly back to L.A. on Wednesday afternoons and start the process all over again. It meant that they were only apart for a couple of days a week, but with the time difference and the travel headaches, it was an exhausting arrangement.

Erin was also quickly loosing the ability to control her libido but she wouldn't push Abby to give in to the passion that would so easily consume them. She knew Abby would cave if she even suspected how difficult this was becoming for her but she also suspected Abby might have regrets afterwards and she didn't want that.

It was Friday afternoon and Erin was nervous. Despite the fact that she had seen Abby only two days earlier and that they had talked on the phone several times since then, she still held onto the fear that Abby would keep running. That maybe she wouldn't come back. Being apart from her only served to reinforce the fear she was feeling. Her endless days and sleepless nights were filled with nothing but thoughts and dreams of a possible life together.

The sight of Abby walking through the front door of the club was almost unnerving. Just knowing she was there filled the void in her heart. Abby made her whole. Her heart began pounding in her chest as Abby approached and suddenly she could see nothing but the woman she loved. The world around her disappeared and while they embraced there were no sounds, there were no people; there was just the two of them. "I've missed you so much."

"I've missed you too," Abby replied. *More than I can ever tell you.* The enormous loss she had been feeling since Wednesday was instantly gone and everything was right again with the world.

Abby had decided earlier that morning that she was ready to take things to the next level with Erin and she had been incredibly excited about it ever since. She couldn't wait for Erin's shift to be over so that she could tell her.

It was at some point on their way up the stairs that Abby's need and desire turned into fear and nervousness. Nervousness? What reason did she have to be nervous? She had been with countless women before Erin, but never had she felt the flutter of butterflies in the pit of her stomach before. Now though, just a few steps away from the pleasure that surely awaited her, she felt woefully inadequate. She knew how to pleasure a woman, it was something she did so often it was almost without thought and perhaps that was the root of her fear.

She had always provided pleasure in the sexual sense of the word, but she had never made love to someone. Erin was special—it would not suffice to simply please her. No, she would have to make love to her. The thought both fascinated and terrified Abby at the same time. Making love would mean totally and completely giving herself to this woman. Giving her heart, her mind, her body, and her soul. The body part was easy. It was her heart, mind and soul that she had never given to anyone before. She had spent her entire life trying to protect herself from this very thing. Her casual encounters, her rules—it all seemed so simple back then. But back then, was before Erin, and nothing in her life had been simple since the day she met her.

As she stood in front of that same picture window looking out into the city she finally found the courage to say the words that Erin had been waiting so long to hear.

"Erin," Abby said softly, meeting her compassionate gaze. "Make me yours."

Erin was shocked. Over the last several weeks, she had struggled to uphold her agreement to wait, and now, when she least expected it, Abby was ready.

"Are you sure?" she asked hesitantly.

"I'm sure I love you, so yes, I'm ready," she replied honestly.

"Say it again," Erin pleaded.

"I love you." Abby was shocked at how easily the words left her mouth. She could say them over and over again.

With trembling hands, she guided Abby to the bedroom and slowly undressed her, kissing her the entire time. Erin was in awe of the beautiful perfection that was Abby. Her body was more exquisite than she had imagined; rock solid, but soft and supple in all the right places. She had felt Abby close to her and had an idea of what she would look like naked, but she had never anticipated such perfection. "Abby, you are amazing," she said as her greedy eyes took in the sight of Abby's naked body and gently guided her down onto the bed.

It took every ounce of self-control she had not to ravish her that very instant. She had planned for this night to be perfect; for it to be just about pleasing Abby and she wanted it to be slow and sensual. She wanted it to take hours, but Abby's body was causing her to lose control of her own. She didn't know how long Abby had been stroking her nipples while they kissed, but when she finally made the connection in her mind, she firmly gripped Abby's hand and stopped her. "Stop please!" she managed to say in short gasping breaths. "I want ..." she struggled for words, her throat dry with excitement and hunger "I want to please you tonight," she finally regained her composure long enough to explain. "I want tonight to be about you and only you. I don't want any distractions."

Abby looked at her questioningly, remembering the way Lauren had used sex to control her. She did not want to go down that road again. But when she looked into Erin's eyes, she saw that this was not about control, it was about pleasure. It was a gift. For Erin to put her own needs aside for the night to please Abby was a remarkable sacrifice and Abby would not forget it. No one had ever done this for her before.

With that knowledge, Abby let go of her insecurities and she allowed herself to enjoy this precious gift. This woman was truly somewhat of a mystery to Abby. A beautiful, wonderful, terrifying mystery.

Erin made her way painstakingly slowly down the length of Abby's body. Taking the time to gently fondle and caress every inch of her from the top of her head to the tips of her toes. She kept her eyes locked on Abby's the whole time; memorizing every little spot of Abby's body that seemed to enjoy her touch, the tender place behind her knees, the sensitive flesh above her hip bone; so many places to explore and enjoy.

"Erin, I don't think I can take much more of this; I think I'm going to explode," Abby begged. Erin smiled, but did not respond, as she continued her assault of Abby's body. Her tongue tracing the gentle recesses of Abby's six-pack abs. The feel of her muscles quivering beneath her touch caused a fury of excitement and satisfaction she had never before experienced.

Abby was growing restless. Her need for release was overpowering. She pleaded with Erin again. Noticing a look of desperation on Abby's face that she had never seen before on any woman caused Erin to tremble. She wasn't ready to stop yet, but she was powerless against Abby's pleading.

"Okay, darling," Erin said as she gently rolled off of Abby and removed her clothes quickly and easily before lowering herself back down on top of her and bringing their lips together for a deep meaningful kiss.

Her hands quickly travelled to Abby's breasts, fingers nimbly stroking and pulling at her erect nipples. Unfocussed, caught up in wild abandon, Abby tangled her fingers in Erin's hair and gently pushed her down toward her breasts. Erin eagerly sucked and flicked the pert nipple with her tongue bringing Abby even higher. The sounds of appreciation, combined with the feeling of Abby's hot wet arousal against her skin nearly caused Erin to lose control. A few more minutes of this and she herself would come unwillingly.

Struggling to maintain focus, Erin slid her hand the length of Abby's body and explored the silky wet flesh around her clit before bringing her fingers to her mouth sensually to suck the sweet juices from them. Abby moaned again, her body writhing beneath Erin's with a need so great she was certain something was certainly going to explode if she didn't have contact soon. "Now please!" she ordered.

Erin obliged by returning her fingers to Abby's clit. "You're so wet! So beautiful like this," she whispered between kisses before making her way down Abby's body so her mouth could join her fingers. Immediately upon first contact, Abby's body tensed and she arched and pushed herself hard against Erin's mouth. Erin knew it was too soon, but there was no turning back now. She struggled to keep Abby still as she fought to break the contact, which was much too intense while she rolled Abby's hard clit between her lips and tugged playfully for several minutes until she could feel the first waves of Abby's orgasm washing over her.

The more Abby tried to pull away, the harder she sucked until finally Abby cried out, a kaleidoscope of colors flashed before her eyes, her rigid body lifted off the bed, for what felt like minutes, she was unable to draw breath and then she fell limply back down in pure exhaustion. A multitude of fascinating sensations, unlike anything she had ever experienced before, passed through her. Indescribable warmth enveloped her and when she was finally able to open her eyes, the ones that met hers were full of love.

Although she had never seen the look before, she knew the look in Erin's eyes was love. She reached up to stroke Erin's cheek and urged her forward so their lips could meet in a soft gentle kiss that spoke wordlessly of the love they both felt. "I love you."

"I love you too. Now, get some sleep. You're going to need your rest for what I have planned for tomorrow," Erin replied before pulling Abby into her arms.

They remained that way, gazing hopelessly into each other's eyes for several minutes until both women drifted off into a blissful sleep.

A few hours later, Abby woke and smiled when she realized that she was in Erin's bed and was suddenly very aroused as the memory of their earlier encounter flooded her mind. She rolled over to catch the beautiful sight of Erin sleeping peacefully next to her. She had a most content look on her face. *She can't be real, can she?* She didn't want to wake her, but she just had to touch her to make sure she was real. She reached over and was just about to touch her cheek when Erin smiled; eye's still closed, but very much awake.

"Hi!" she said dreamily.

"I didn't mean to wake you ... I was just watching you sleep and ..." Abby teasingly traced small circles on Erin's chest with her fingers. "Looking at you makes me feel all warm and tingly inside."

"Is that a good thing?" Erin asked.

"It's wonderful!" Abby rested her head on Erin's shoulder, wrapped her arm around her waist, and let out a long, peaceful breath. Content for now just to be in Erin's arms, hearing and feeling her breath on her face, she drifted off to sleep.

"Aunt Erin," Meg shouted as she pounded on her aunt's bedroom door.

"Go away!" Erin shouted back, content to remain right were she was nestled into Abby's breasts.

"I need to talk to you," Meg pleaded.

"I have company," Erin replied in the sternest voice she could manage.

"I know. Good morning, Abby. I'm sorry, but I need to talk to Aunt Erin right away," she pleaded again through the bedroom door.

"Fine!" Erin conceded. "Give me five minutes and there had better be coffee."

Abby smiled and began to get out of bed but Erin pulled her back down and began tracing small circles over her stomach. "You are unbelievably responsive," Erin said watching Abby's body react to her touch.

"What do you mean?" she questioned.

"Watch." Erin teased, passing her finger over Abby's nipple without touching it. They were both awed at the fact that it hardened and swelled in anticipation of her touch. "See what I mean. I don't even have to touch you."

Abby wiggled away again remembering Meg's pleas. "You had better get out there. She's waiting."

"I know, but this, would be so much more fun," Erin said while kissing Abby's stomach sensually.

"Erin, please!" Abby begged, unsure if it sounded more like please stop or please don't stop.

"Please what?" Erin replied teasingly, stroking the delicate skin on Abby's thigh.

"You have to stop. God, I wish you wouldn't, but you have to," Abby pleaded again.

"Okay, okay," Erin said getting out of bed. "I'll be back in a few minutes, don't go anywhere."

"I wouldn't dream of leaving this spot."

As soon as Erin left the room, Abby got up, took a quick shower and changed the sheets before returning to the spot she said she wouldn't leave.

"What could be so important that you had to drag me away from the one and only thing I was planning to do today?" Erin asked impatiently.

"I did something stupid," Meg said as calmly as possible.

"Stupider than getting me out of bed this morning?"

"I kissed Stephanie."

Erin was silent for a few minutes. She walked over to the counter, poured herself a cup of coffee and took several sips, trying to wake up from the sex-induced coma she felt like she was in, long enough to process what she just heard.

"Would you mind repeating what you just said? I can't possibly have heard you correctly."

"I said I kissed Stephanie."

Erin banged her head repeatedly against the cupboard door in frustration.

"What are you doing?" Meg asked.

"I'm trying to dislodge whatever it is that's keeping me from hearing you right."

"This isn't funny, I need your help." Meg was near tears and her aunt's attempts at making a joke of her situation were only making things worse.

"Sit down, Megan," Erin said seriously. "Before I start lecturing you, why don't you tell me what happened."

"I don't know exactly. We were sitting there talking and then, I just kissed her. It just happened."

"How did she react?"

"I don't know. I ran out of there so fast I don't know what her reaction was."

"Joanne is going to kill me for this. First, I string her along for months on end, and then you decide to play games with her daughter."

"First of all, Joanne has moved on, and secondly, who says I'm playing games. You never asked me how I felt about it."

Erin poured herself another cup of coffee and hesitantly took a seat next to her niece at the kitchen table. She didn't like the direction this conversation taking.

"How do you feel about it?" she asked, despite not wanting to know the answer.

"It was amazing. I don't know how Stephanie feels about it, and that's the really scary part, but I really, really liked it."

"I need to sit down," Erin said despite the fact that she was already sitting down. She felt like she was falling from something very high and was powerless to stop it.

"You are sitting."

"Then I need to lie down." She got up and added a shot of Bailey's to her coffee before returning to the table.

Trying to delay the delicate conversation that was looming, she tried to shift their talk in a different direction. "What's the deal with Joanne?"

"I guess I forgot to tell you that I ran into Dinah a couple weeks ago. She told me she was thinking about selling the house and I decided to give her Joanne's phone number."

"Are you out of your freaking mind?"

"Relax okay. Dinah's got her shit together. If she hadn't, I wouldn't have encouraged the two of them. Last night was their first real date, but Dinah's car was still in the driveway when I left this morning."

"Are you trying to kill me?"

"Not intentionally." She smiled. "Now, are you going to help me, or what?"

"I choose, *or what*." She laughed and pulled her niece into a giant bear hug.

"Get away from me. And take a shower. You smell like sex."

"I should. What did you think you were interrupting this morning? Did you think I was in there reading her bedtime stories or something?"

"Ew! Gross. T.M.I."

"Do you really think I want to hear about how much you liked kissing Stephanie?"

"Point taken. Now, what do I do?"

"Your only choice, if you want to have any kind of relationship with her at all, even if it's just a friendship, is to march back over there and apologize. How does Chloe fit into all of this?"

"They broke up a couple of days ago."

"Don't push Steph, Megan. No matter how you feel about her. Give it some time."

"I'll try." She kissed her aunt on the cheek and made her way to the door. "Seriously, take a shower."

# Chapter Twenty-One

Erin took Megan's advice and took a quick shower before returning to the warmth of Abby's naked body in her bed. She stopped dead in her tracks when she saw that Abby was fast asleep. She was sure she had never seen such a beautiful sight. She decided that waking her would be rude and she didn't think she could remain still if she returned to the bed, so she quietly left the room.

About an hour later, a fully rested and fully dressed, Abby emerged from the bedroom, poured herself a cup of coffee and joined Erin at the kitchen table.

"Good morning," Abby said and placed a gentle kiss on Erin's lips.

"I could definitely get used to this," Erin replied, enjoying the taste of Abby's lips.

"Did you get enough sleep?"

"I think that should last me for a couple of days," Abby replied seductively.

"Well then," Erin said as she took Abby's hand. "Let's pick up where we left off before we were so rudely interrupted."

"Is everything all right with Meg?" she asked genuinely concerned.

"Let's not let my niece's raging hormones, interfere with my raging hormones anymore today. I'll tell you all about it some other time."

Abby reached up to meet Erin's lips and kissed her softly at first, savouring their taste. As the kiss grew, Abby felt she was losing herself once again. Although she cherished the way she felt when Erin kissed her, she secretly wished that the effect would be less debilitating. When Erin kissed her, her knees grew weak, her head began to spin, and she was lost in the clouds that seemingly filled the room around them, unable to think rationally or function. They remained in that embrace for several minutes taking the time to enjoy the moment until Erin, much to Abby's dismay and relief broke away from the kiss.

"Take me to my bed," she ordered.

Abby smiled and led her to the bedroom where, once inside, their lips reunited once again. She took her time slowly removing Erin's tank top, exposing her beautiful full breasts. She kissed her flat stomach as she unbuttoned her jeans and pushed them to the floor with her panties. Abby stepped away taking in the sight "You're stunningly beautiful," she said before removing her own shirt and jeans; remaining in her bra and panties, to try to retain some sense of control over her own reaction.

She gently urged Erin down on the bed beneath her and spent a few moments caressing the tender skin just above Erin's collarbone before speaking. "Roll over."

"What?" Erin replied

"Roll over. Don't you trust me?" Abby asked coyly.

"It's not a matter of trust, darling. I'm dying over here. I need you. I can't wait much longer." Abby's hot, wet lips, immediately silenced her.

"Just roll over. I want to spend a little bit of time getting to know my favourite part of your body first. Besides, it's the least you could do considering the slow torture you bestowed on me last night."

"Oh, I see, so this is revenge for last night. So, that's the way we're going to play, huh? Okay, but just remember fair is fair." She chuckled before finally rolling over onto her stomach.

Abby wasted no time getting acquainted with the smooth flesh that had been calling to her since they first met. She knew that most women were into breasts, asses or legs, but not Abby; she was into shoulders. Perfect shoulders that were toned and broad enough to create the beautiful vee shape down to their waists. Women had to work very hard to get that physique, but not Erin; she was born with it and Abby loved it.

She wasn't sure how long she had spent caressing the tender flesh, biting it, teasing it, but Erin's body was writhing beneath her, calling to her. She reached one hand between the mattress and Erin's body finding an erect nipple between her fingers. Erin instantly moaned and propped herself up on her elbows wanting more, needing more.

"Please Abby, I need to come," she said desperately. Abby smiled in awe of the fact that she had caused this amazing woman to reach a desire so deep it caused her to beg.

"You will, when I'm ready to let you," Abby teased, biting Erin's neck just hard enough to leave a mark. Erin bucked in response trying to throw Abby off of her, but quickly surrendered when Abby's hand finally reached her soft, pulsating mound. Abby teased for a moment, stroking delicately around her swollen clit causing Erin to feel faint and foggy. Her breathing was rapid, her body tense. She was quickly nearing the edge and Abby knew it. She danced around it, holding her captive right on the edge. Abby wanted to see her face when she came so she quickly removed her hand causing Erin to whimper.

"Roll over, I want to watch you," Abby urged.

"I don't ... I can't ... God! Abby, what did you do to me?" Erin replied trying to urge herself to roll over. Abby, sensing Erin's inability to function on her own gently pulled her over onto her back.

"Erin, open your eyes please."

Erin was surprised at the tenderness she saw in Abby's eyes. It was something she didn't expect from her. She wondered how many other wonderful things she would learn about the woman loved.

"Do you want me to make you come now?" Abby asked in a deep, throaty voice.

Erin willed herself to answer, but all she could do was moan, her body was no longer her own. She belonged to Abby, whatever she wanted she would give her.

Abby was hungry, her mouth feasting on the sweet taste of Erin's skin. Abby pushed her own needs aside for the time being, and focussed on nothing but the beautiful woman beneath her.

Erin's eyes were demanding and desperate as Abby's mouth made its way to her breast. Her tongue flicking at the taut nipple, sending her higher. As she took the nipple into her mouth, she bit down gently and slipped two fingers inside, sending her once again to the edge. Knowing she was teetering on the brink and one wrong move would send her over, Abby removed her fingers and her tongue trailed a path from her chest down her smooth stomach, circling her navel before teasing the swollen throbbing lips.

Abby was lost in her scent; it entranced her. She wrapped her arms around Erin's thighs pinning her to the bed, so she could feast on the sweet, flowing juices that waited. Her tongue was at odds with her brain as the fight between her desire to please slowly and her own need to take raged on. She used long, slow strokes carefully avoiding the Erin's delicate clit. She derived great pleasure from watching Erin's body respond seemingly out of control. She was flailing about, her hands tugging desperately at the sheets, pulling them off the bed. Abby used all the force she had to hold Erin down on the bed as she finally took her. Her body completely out of control as Abby's mouth sucked her clit, teasing it with her teeth. Abby was relentless as the first waves of Erin's orgasm hit. She continued her assault taking more; wanting more, not yet satisfied she slipped a finger inside seeking her G-spot. Within seconds, Erin fell limply on the bed and Abby smiled; satisfied in knowing that she had been the one to cause such pleasure. She lay still, gently caressing Erin's stomach, until the beautiful woman finally opened her eyes.

She was barely able to keep them open. Her body felt heavy and lifeless, but she felt more alive than she had ever felt in her life.

"Hey, you okay?" Abby whispered.

"Jesus, Abby!" Erin replied, still trying to catch her breath. Never in her wildest dreams did she think that she could feel this way. No one had ever caused her to lose complete control and she had never wanted to, until now. Something in the way Abby looked at her made her feel safe. Something deeper than the desire and need in her eyes; there was a knowing softness; a sweet tenderness like no other.

"Did I hurt you?" Abby responded horrified, replaying the encounter, trying to remember exactly what she had done. She knew she had been gentle, but there were a few moments of unbridled bliss that she could not recall.

"No," Erin replied quickly. "You didn't hurt me." *Not yet anyway*, she thought to herself knowing that Abby owned her heart and there was no turning back. She was in love. There was no denying it. Abby, still puzzled, looked into her eyes, searching for truth. Erin scooped Abby into her arms and gazed into her eyes. "I love you, Abigail Grant." Before Abby could respond, Erin kissed her.

"I'm home! And I brought dinner." Meg shouted from the kitchen startling the two women who were in a world of their own.

"We'll be right out!" Erin shouted back trying to figure out how to avoid the soon to be uncomfortable situation. "Shit!" she whispered to Abby. "We have to take a shower before dinner. Do you think you can keep your hands to yourself?" Erin added with a chuckle.

Abby was on her best behaviour. Erin was the one who couldn't keep her hands from exploring Abby's naked body. By the time their shower was over, Abby was completely aroused and frustrated.

"You're going to pay for this, you know," she joked as the two headed to the kitchen to join Meg.

"I look forward to it," Erin replied with a seductive smile.

"Pay for what?" Meg asked innocently.

"Nothing," the two women answered with a giggle in unison.

They enjoyed a quick dinner with Meg, who seemed to be in a much better mood, before abruptly leaving the table and heading back to the bedroom.

"Wait! Stop!" Abby said just as Erin's mouth reached its target.

"What? You seemed to like it yesterday as I recall," she said looking up at Abby with a hurt and confused look on her face.

"Come up here for a minute," Abby said softly.

"What's wrong?" Erin asked now very concerned.

"Nothing," Abby said brushing the hair from Erin's eyes. "I need to feel you. I need to see you. I want your body against mine," she said desperately.

"Are you sure, Abby? I don't know if I can control myself enough not to hurt you," she said, remembering how many times she had gotten carried away in situations like this.

"Quite frankly, if a bruised pelvis will keep me from wanting to have sex with you tomorrow while I'm at work; I will consider it a blessing."

Erin looked at her hesitantly, pondering the thought. "Okay. If you're sure. But you get on top," she said struggling to flip them over, but Abby was too strong. Despite Erin's longer limbs, her leverage was no match for Abby's strength.

"Not a chance," Abby said smiling through her satisfaction.

Erin reached between them and spread her swollen tender lips to expose her hypersensitive clitoris. Abby followed suit just before Erin lowered herself. The moment of contact was almost too much to bear for both women as they struggled to hold back their raging orgasms. They both moaned with pleasure, but neither of them moved for a very long time until the sensation passed. Abby was first to begin the slow, steady roll of her hips, but it wasn't long before Erin joined in, matching her rhythm perfectly.

Their mouths met with such ferocity that it was as if they were trying to draw breath from each other. As their orgasms neared, the slow, steady rocking of their intimate dance was replaced with hard, deliberate collisions. Sensing Erin was holding back, Abby opened her eyes to provide reassurance to the questioning ones looking back at her. With that, Erin let herself go; no longer concerned about the pain she began bucking wildly, taking control of satisfying her own needs. She was close and Abby's fingernails pressing into the flesh on her back left little doubt that she was far behind. One last thrust sent them both over the edge but to both of their surprise, the mutual sensation of each other's pleasure resulted in a renewed arousal "I'm going to … again!" Abby managed through ragged breaths. "Me too … Can't stop" Erin said trying to control her third orgasm.

Both women, completely spent, lay motionless, revelling in the after shocks flowing through their bodies. Only when she thought she had finally found her voice did Abby manage to say, "Wow!"

"Mmm. That's what I was going to say. I've never …" Erin said as she delicately rolled onto her side next to Abby. She was glad that she had turned the stereo on to muffle the sounds coming out of her room so Meg wouldn't hear them.

"Me neither," Abby replied still breathless from the exertion. "Are you sleepy, baby?"

"Very. Is that okay?" she asked fearful that Abby was anything but sleepy.

"Absolutely okay," she mumbled totally exhausted sitting up to put on a t-shirt and panties, knowing that if she didn't they wouldn't get any sleep at all. Erin did the same and settled back down onto the bed with her back to Abby. Abby wrapped her arm around Erin's waist, slipped her thumb beneath the waistband of her panties, and rested it there. A possessive gesture. A simple gesture. Yet a gesture so meaningful, that it caused Erin's eyes to well up with tears. *Yes, Abby, I'm yours,* she thought to herself, as she drifted into a sound sleep.

"Are you sure you're ready for this?" Erin asked as they climbed on her bike the following Saturday afternoon.

"Yes," Abby lied. She was nowhere near ready to meet Erin's family, but she knew it was important to Erin, so she would find a way to cope with the uncertainty she was feeling.

"It's too bad Meg had to work. I'm sure her little coming out announcement would have saved me from some of the scrutiny I'm about to be subjected to."

"It wouldn't have helped. My mom has been bugging me to bring you over since I made the mistake of mentioning that I was seeing you a few weeks ago. Trust me. This is going to be worse for me, than it is for you."

After a wonderful evening with Erin's family, they crawled into her small twin childhood bed and Abby quickly found herself on top of Erin showering her with kisses. It had been a long week and an even longer day being so close to her without being able to touch her. The simple caresses that passed between them during the day served simply to fan the still-glowing embers from the weekend before. "Abby stop," Erin said struggling to pull away from Abby's kisses long enough to speak.

"What? I'll be quiet. I promise," Abby replied before capturing Erin's mouth again with hers.

"No. It's not that," Erin replied, escaping again to gain Abby's attention. "I can't." she paused slightly embarrassed. "It's my time of the month."

"Oh. Sorry. I didn't even think about that. I have such a low body fat content, I hardly ever get mine any more." Abby was caught completely off guard by Erin's admission. She had never been faced with this situation before. She gave Erin a quick kiss and gently rolled herself over onto her back so that they found themselves both on their backs, looking up at the ceiling.

"Are you going to be okay? If you want I can ..." Erin started to say when Abby silenced her.

"Shh. I'm fine. Come here," she said as she lifted her arm for Erin to curl in next to her then wrapped it tightly around her. Erin rested her head on the younger woman's shoulder, wrapped her arm around her waist and draped her leg over Abby's thigh and was suddenly filled with an overwhelming sense of peace. Never again did she want to be anywhere but lying in Abby's arms.

The urge to touch her was more than she could stand so she gently began running her fingers teasingly over Abby's abdomen feeling the muscles ripple beneath them until Abby reached out her hand to stop her.

"Sorry. I like to touch you," she said innocently.

"Mmm. I like it when you touch me, but please, I can't take it," Abby replied all the while trying to conjure up terrible thoughts to keep herself from getting aroused.

"It's kind of a big deal that I'm here with you this weekend isn't it?" Abby questioned thinking of the big fuss Erin's family had made over her and how nervous Erin had been all day.

"It's a very big deal," Erin admitted knowing that she had never brought a woman home with her for the weekend. Although Dinah occasionally joined them for Sunday dinner, she had never once spent the night. It was a bigger deal than Abby would ever know.

"Thank you." She somehow felt honoured at having been invited to not only meet Erin's family, but to join in with them in what could only be described as ritualistic behaviour. From what she had learned, this was a weekly occurrence in the Davis household, and although Erin could only get a weekend off here or there to participate, it was clearly important to her. Each family member seemed to have their own responsibility when it came time to preparing meals and tending to chores and Abby was more than pleased to take on Meg's responsibilities this weekend while she was at work. She wondered what it might have been like if her family had been more like Erin's.

"Your family is very friendly. I like them a lot."

"They seem to like you very much, too. I'm very happy about that." *Because I want you to come with me everywhere I go from now on*; she wanted to say, but was afraid to add.

"Erin! Erin wake up!" she said shaking her gently from sleep.

"What?" she mumbled without opening her eyes.

"Good morning, Mrs. Davis," Abby said to the woman standing in the doorway looking at them with a puzzled look on her face.

"Mom. What do you want?" Erin asked finally awake, embarrassed to know that her mother had found her with her head resting on Abby's breast.

"Just came to let you girls know breakfast will be ready in fifteen minutes," she said cheerily as she left the room and closed the door behind her.

"Oh my God. I'm so embarrassed."

"I suppose it could have been worse." Abby giggled. "We could have been naked." With that, they both laughed. Abby found herself admiring yet another facet of Erin's personality: one that was afraid of her mother. "I can't imagine ever loving you more than I love you right now, but somehow, I'm sure I will," Abby said wrapping her arms around Erin's shoulders and kissing her on the top of her head.

"This doesn't get any easier," Abby said when they arrived at the airport for her return flight home. The weekend had been wonderful, but much too short. There was so much more she wanted to tell Erin, so many emotions she wanted to share, but there was never enough time. Erin was getting too busy, with the new club opening soon, to be able to fly back to Michigan with her during the week, so they wouldn't see each other again until the following weekend.

"What doesn't, darling?"

"Leaving you."

"Then stay," Erin said simply as if it was a viable option.

"You know I have to work tomorrow," she said as she held Erin's hands and swung her arms playfully to impede the imminent sadness.

"I mean forever. I love you," Erin replied softly, looking into Abby's eyes.

*Did she just ask me to move in with her? It's too soon; I must have heard her wrong.* Abby did not respond to Erin's statement for fear that she had misunderstood. "I love you too. I'll call you when I get in."

As she walked away, she replayed the conversation over and over again in her mind. Maybe she really did hear what she thought she heard. If so, was it even possible?

# *Epilogue*

"I can't believe she's giving this place up," Toni exclaimed to Hailey.

"It's amazing isn't it?" Hailey replied with a sigh as she glanced around Abby's house. "I remember the first night I met her. She was so determined to never fall in love that she even had a rule about never sleeping with the same woman twice."

Toni shook her head in disbelief and looked out the window at Erin and Abby who were standing in the driveway gazing hopelessly into each other's eyes. "And look at her now."

"Yeah, she's in deep. I've never seen two happier people in my life … I'm going to miss her though." Hailey was torn between wanting her best friend to be happy and the loss she was feeling

"I know, baby, but we'll visit them, I promise," Toni said reassuringly.

"I know, but it won't be the same. And I can't believe she's letting us live here. What are we going to do with all of this space?"

"I'm sure will figure something out," Toni replied and pulled Hailey to her as they watched Erin and Abby put the final boxes in the car.

An early November snow had begun to fall and Abby took one last breath of cool Michigan air before getting into the car. She knew she was making the right decision.

"Are you okay, darling?" Erin asked as she looked over at Abby sitting quietly in the passenger seat.

"I've never been better." She reached over and took Erin's hand in hers, certain for the first time in her life, that this was what she wanted. "I love you. I can't wait to spend the rest of my life with you."

978-0-595-70710-2
0-595-70710-6

Lightning Source UK Ltd.
Milton Keynes UK
18 November 2009
146439UK00002B/18/A